Kei

The Death Sentence

A Detective Inspector Batt thriller

Copyright © 2025 Keith A Baker

ISBN: 978-1-917601-84-9

All rights reserved, including the right to reproduce this book, or portions thereof in any form. No part of this text may be reproduced, transmitted, downloaded, decompiled, reverse engineered, or stored, in any form or introduced into any information storage and retrieval system, in any form or by any means, whether electronic or mechanical without the express written permission of the author.

This is a work of fiction. Names and characters are the product of the author's imagination and any resemblance to actual persons, living or dead, is entirely coincidental.

The views expressed in this work are solely those of the author and do not necessarily reflect the views of the publisher, and the publisher hereby disclaims any responsibility for them.

To Margo and Al
xxx

Chapter 1

Detective Inspector Batt had not been best pleased when his phone had woken him at 8:00am. He'd only recently arrived home having done a late shift at the Station in nearby Burton-on-Trent. Whether it had been the unusually prolonged spell of hot weather, or the strong smell of hops that hung over the town, he couldn't tell, but people seemed to be a good deal more confrontational than usual. During the course of the shift he had been called out to several skirmishes and allegations of threatening behaviour and, quite frankly, he had had enough and was glad when it had been time to hand over to DI Mills. It was more his cup of tea. Batt had grown tired of the "Eastenders" mentality that seemed to have taken a hold on society. It was the pettiness of it all that got to him. Everyone felt it their right to interfere in everybody else's business. Someone doing something you didn't like? Get your phone out, film it and stick it on Facebook for others to add their sixpennyworth.

So when his phone had rung he hadn't been particularly civil to DC Talbot.

'This better be a matter of life or death, Chris.'

'Death, Sir,' had been the reply.

'Go on. And don't tell me it's some kiddie's pet hamster or I will remove its wheel from its cage and insert it...'

'No Sir,' Talbot had interrupted before the exact location of the wheel could be made known, 'a suspicious death at Fairview Mansions. It was called in about half an hour ago. I think you'll be the Investigating Officer, Sir.'

Batt had managed a few mouthfuls of the sawdust they called muesli before grabbing a banana from the bowl in the kitchen and setting off on the twenty-minute drive back to Burton.

By the time he'd reached the village of Newborough he'd calmed down enough to put a CD of Annie Lennox into the car's player. Annie Lennox, Carole King, Dusty Springfield – particularly Dusty Springfield – they could be guaranteed to raise your spirits. And right now, heading for Fairview Mansions, his spirits definitely needed a boost.

Fairview Mansions was, in anybody's book, a misnomer. The only view was of the council tip on one side and a wasteland on the other that the council had planned to redevelop before it had run out of money. Neither view could be called "fair". As for the "Mansions" reference... How many mansions were built to look like a drab, grey concrete box? And its tenants could by no stretch of the imagination be described as members of the aristocracy.

He reached the town hall and joined the one-way system, heading towards Derby Turn. A long row of Victorian terraces, mostly cheap rentals, was on his left and to his right were various cut-price retail units.

Batt took a left turn and parked his car in a side street. He sat for a moment, listening to the end of "There Must Be An Angel" and ejected the CD.

He locked the car and made his way round the corner where he was met with the usual mix of blue flashing lights and police tape. A small crowd had gathered, held back from the block of council flats by the line of police tape. Several had their phones held aloft, filming events for social media.

'Nothing like a sunny day and a crime scene for bringing out the masses,' he thought.

It was the start of what the weather forecasters had predicted would be a long spell of settled weather, with record September temperatures likely. DI Batt had developed a dislike for hot weather ever since his army days spent in the stifling heat of Afghanistan. He'd never experienced anything like it, not helped of course by the 54Kg of body armour that each soldier had to wear as protection against Taliban attacks. He tried to dismiss the memory. This was a housing estate in Burton-on-Trent, not a compound just outside Musa Qaleh. Mind you, he reflected, both communities eyed him with a degree of suspicion. Just as it had been in 2008, so it was now in 2024: a battle for hearts and minds.

'Hi Mr Batt,' called a youth sitting astride a bike with ridiculously small wheels. He beckoned Batt over with a turn of his head.

When Batt was alongside , the youth asked if he'd been able to get hold of a new set of nets for the youth club pitch.

'They'll be with you shortly, Dean. Just waiting for the sarge to get down to "Sports Are Us". Mind you, he's not lightning quick on his pins so I may have to go myself. You still keeping out of trouble?'

'Yes Mr Batt. The youth club leader wants me to go in for my junior coaching badges.'

'Nice one Dean. You'll make a good coach. Saw your mum in B&M the other day. She enjoying her job?'

'Yes. Thanks for helping her Mr Batt. She's not drinking as much since she started. And she's taking me and Kira to Alton Towers on Saturday.'

'What's the drug situation round your neck of the woods?'

'Better since the Donoghues were kicked out.'

'Well, keep your eyes open for me, Dean. You know how it is – one dealer goes and another takes his place.'

'I will, Mr Batt.'

He was getting ready to cycle off when Batt stopped him.

'By the way, why aren't you in school?'

'Teachers on strike again. We ain't got to go in until this afternoon.'

'But you've only just got back from the summer holidays.'

'I know, Mr Batt. It's great isn't it. Anyways I'd best get going. I'm off to Makies to get our Kira something for her lunch. See you Mr Batt.'

'Take care lad.'

He watched Dean do a wheelie and disappear round the corner of the building but before he could duck under the police tape he was intercepted by one of the "Burton Star's" reporters.

'George. Thought I'd see you on scene. Anything you can tell me?" she asked, holding up a dictaphone.

'Put it away, Lucy. The only thing I can tell you' and he dropped his voice to a whisper, 'is that my breakfast hasn't had time to go down yet. Give me a ring later and I'll see what I can do.'

'Thanks George – appreciate it. By the way, what do you make of your new Chief Constable?'

'Haven't had the pleasure yet.'

'She was on the tv breakfast news. Got the power dressing off to a tee. Seems to have a bee in her bonnet about clearing up hate crimes. She's appealed to anyone who feels they have been abused to come forward.'

Batt raised his eyes to the heavens, visualising the stream of nutters and loners who would no doubt be filing complaints at this very minute, taking officers' time away from the genuine cases.

'Yes, well, the Commissioner doesn't like to be responsible for a failing Force. He's apparently seeking re-election in May. Sees the new Chief as someone who can help him achieve his aims. And no, you can't quote me. How's the puppy. Got him house trained yet?'

'He's coming on. Seems to have taken a liking to the dining table legs. He's almost gnawed through one of them. Richie says it's because he's teething.'

'You'll have to bring him round to the Station. We've got a dog handler who can give you a few tips. Mind you he does tend to know more about Alsations that poodles.'

The Murder Investigation Team team had evidently seen as much as they wanted and were standing around outside the main entrance to the block, some removing their white coveralls and others sipping coffee from styrofoam cups.

'George,' called one of them, 'how's things?'

Batt walked over to him. 'Could be better. Got a new Inspector who is on a mission.'

'What's he like?'

'He's a she, and I've yet to be introduced. Word has it she intends to clean up our act and turn us all into proper police officers. What have we got?'

'White male, probably in his sixties, with a hole in his head. Probably been dead for a day or so – he's just starting to go off. Not a pleasant smell, and this heat hasn't helped. Place is a tip but no signs of a forced entry and nothing much for the forensics to investigate. Siobhan's still up there. Our lovely pathologist will be able to tell you more. Top floor.'

He crumpled his cup and tossed it in through the open door of a waiting Transit.

'Worth calling in the PolSA team?'

'Not really. Nothing much for them to look for apparently.'

Batt made his way to the main door and showed his ID to a bored-looking constable.

'I'm Batt, Crime Scene Manager, and button your collar up, lad, you'll be starring in social media before the end of the morning. Can't have the Force looking scruffy with the world looking on. Images been yet?'

'Yes Sir. Been and gone.'

'They don't hang about, do they!'

'Wednesday, Sir. Full English in the canteen on Wednesdays, Sir.'

Batt sighed and made his way into the building to be greeted by the usual stomach-turner of fresh curry and disinfectant.

And the usual sight of an out-of-order lift.

He sighed and began the long haul up the concrete stairs.

'Why is it always on the top floor?' he thought, 'and why do they always paint the stairwells in that awful public toilet green? No wonder it gets used as one.'

He was met at the top by his keen new DC.

'Ah Sir,' he said, 'I've been waiting for you.'

'Think I've pulled a muscle,' replied Batt. 'Come on then. MIT have gone. It's safe to enter.'

Batt produced two sets of coveralls, over-shoes, masks, hair nets and nitrile gloves.

'Here put these on. Two pairs of gloves, mind, just to make sure you don't come into contact with any nasty fluids. Never know if forensics have missed something. Oh and use a dab of this before you put your mask on. Apparently the body has started to self digest.'

He produced a tub of Vic and went through the open door of the flat breathing through his mouth. There was a sweet, sickly smell but nowhere near as bad as Batt had encountered at previous scenes of death.

The room was a mess of empty lager cans and discarded clothes. A few stepping plates had been left in place by the investigation team. The smell was vile.

Siobhan Jackson was dictating notes into her phone and signalled Batt over to a body lying sprawled in a battered armchair. His clothes had seen better days and his hair clearly hadn't been cut in months. As murder victims went this one was not one to make him want to say hello to his breakfast again. There was a neat hole in the centre of his forehead that Batt considered shouldn't have been there.

Siobhan finished her monologue and came over.

'Hi Siobhan. This is…' Batt looked round for his DC and found him ashen faced, standing in the doorway. 'Well come in lad, it won't bite. Neither will the corpse.'

'Ha ha,' said Siobhan. 'First murder is it?' she asked DC Talbot, who put his hand to his mask and nodded. 'Keep to the stepping plates.'

He made his way into the room, his eyes fixed on the corpse which was attracting the attention of large black flies.

'Right,' continued Batt. 'Siobhan, this is DC….' and he searched desperately in his memory for a name.

'Talbot,' said Talbot. 'Chris Talbot.'

'And this is our forensic pathologist Dr Siobhan Fahy.'

'Good to meet you Chris. Can we all stand back and wait a few minutes?'

They retreated to the far side of the room. Dr Fahy opened her case and took out her camera and a digital thermometer. She used the thermometer to record the room's temperature. Before long there was a loud buzzing and a swarm of flies settled on the bloated body. They made for the eyes and mouth and seemed to relish the fluids draining from there.

'Blowfly,' she said, and took a few photographs.

She moved over to the body and rooted around.

'Blowfly maggots but no pupae that I can see. This probably means the body has been dead for less than a few days otherwise there would be pupae. In fact, looking at the size of the larger ones,' she continued, moving closer, 'I would say more like a couple of days. A blowfly maggot reaches about one centimeter in length after a couple of days. After four days it becomes a pupa.'

The three of them stood there staring at the heaving mass of maggots devouring the flesh on the victim's head.

'They're fascinating things,' continued Siobhan. 'The maggot shreds decaying flesh with the two hooks in its mouth. It breathes through the opposite end so doesn't need to stop to take a breath. After about four days it will be ten times its original size.'

The pathologist took some close-ups of them before producing a small tin. She went over to the body and picked off some maggots with a pair of tweezers.

'Have you been taught anything about entomology, Chris?'

Talbot shook his head.

'The oldest maggots will help determine when the flies first found the corpse. I'll get them back to the lab and determine what species of blowfly they come from by hatching them out. Different species of blowfly develop at different rates, so it's important I get it right. Knowing the species of blowfly, and establishing the stage of growth of the maggots, should give a pretty good idea of the time of death. I also need to factor in the room temperature because this affects the speed of a maggot's growth. Maggots like to eat a corpse in a sort of feeding frenzy. Shortly before they turn into pupae they can heat that part of a body up to a temperature of fifty degrees.'

She attached a probe to the thermometer and pushed it into the tangle of writhing maggots in the mouth.

'Not especially warm so, as I thought, John Doe has probably been dead for just a couple of days.'

'What if the maggots have turned into pupae?' asked Batt.

'Well, it takes about ten days for a pupa to turn into an adult fly. I can send pupae off to have them put under a small CT scanner. A pupa will not show much development at thirty hours but just three hours later you can see the head, thorax and abdomen developing. It's part of dating a death that we're still researching.'

'Fascinating,' said Talbot, whose interest had seemed to have overcome his nausea.

Batt was using his camera to take photographs from all four corners of the room, putting down more stepping plates as he went before rejoining them at the body.

'Right Chris. What is there a lack of - besides a pulse?'

Talbot considered possibilities but couldn't think of anything.

'He's being put on the graduate fast-track,' said Batt to Siobhan, ' which hopefully means being tied to the HS2 railway line just south of Lichfield. Look again, DC Talbot. What would you expect to see from Fred here who has just been shot in the head?'

'Blood, Sir.'

'Yes, blood. And there isn't any, is there?'

'No Sir.'

'Rigor mortis has come and gone,' said Siobhan. 'Livor mortis in the legs and feet suggests he died in this chair but not, as you say, from the gunshot wound to the head. No obvious signs of ligatures to the wrists or ankles. I'll have a better idea of the time of death when I get him and the maggots back to the mortuary. Do you want to be there when I do the autopsy John?'

'Might be a useful experience for Boy Wonder here.'

'I'll give you a ring in the morning. I've got a train stopper and a suspected over-doser to examine first.'

She collected her things and dodged lightly round the cans as if doing a ballroom dance, making her way to the door.

'I'll tell the ambulance crew to collect in five minutes. Chris,' she said over her shoulder, 'don't let him teach you any of his bad habits. And his bark is worse than his bite.'

When she'd gone Batt studied the body for a moment, telling Talbot to take a further look around the room. He'd seen similar gunshot wounds in Afghanistan. Probably a .38 or .455 calibre. No damage to the back of the seat so whoever had fired the shot had used something like a kevlar pad in order to retrieve the bullet. He'd seen that before, as well.

He moved to the bedroom, took more photographs, and then opened a few drawers and cupboards. In contrast to the living area everything was neat and tidy. Batt looked towards the single bed in the corner and cast an approving eye over the neatly smoothed sheets .When he moved across to the other side of the room and opened a few drawers in the pine chest the clothes were clean, ironed and perfectly laid out. There was a wardrobe alongside. it. He opened the door and found a suit and assorted shirts hanging on the rail. One shirt had fallen off and was lying crumpled on the base. He bent to pick it up and his eye was drawn to a dark straight-line indentation on the carpet just in front of the wardrobe where a previous one had stood.

He looked thoughtful for a moment and walked back through the entrance and into the corridor before turning to look back into the lounge. To a passer-by it would look like an alco's tip – something that wouldn't encourage anyone to want to drop in for a chat.

Batt reached for his phone. From the tinny sound of the ring tone he guessed the pathologist was still in her car. He let it ring until it went through to voice mail.

'Siobhan, it's Batt. Could you do me a favour when you examine Fred and test for alcohol in his system? And drugs,' he added.

He looked round and down as a couple of paramedics clattered up the stairwell.

'He's all yours,' said Batt, removing his protective gear. 'Shame about the lift. Still, easier going down than up I should think. Come on Boy Wonder,' he shouted. 'Time to get back to the station for some lunch. We'll have a debrief this afternoon. Can you get the gang together?

Major Incident Room 2 should be free. We'll meet in there.'

He went out onto the landing and removed his protective gear. He was rolling up his coveralls when the door opposite opened and John Doe's closest neighbour appeared. She was short and overweight and wore a pair of pink shorts that Batt considered a crime worth arresting her for. She eyed him for a moment before yelling over her shoulder something about 'our Jade', 'a packet of biscuits' and 'I'm already late for the bingo'. She turned back to face a smiling Batt.

'Dead is he?' she said, nodding towards the flat across the way. 'Only a matter of time. I'm surprised he didn't do this internal combustion thing the amount he drank.'

'Spontaneous combustion,' he corrected her. 'Drank a lot did he?'

'Well you've been in there," she said moving towards him to get a better view of what was going on through the open door. 'Never without a can in his hand. How he afforded it you tell me. Never known him to do a day's work.'

Batt reached behind him and pulled the door to.

'Drugs, you reckon?'

'Wouldn't be surprised. Not the way things are round here. They're all on drugs. It ain't safe to go out, know what I mean? It's a wonder I ain't been molested before now.'

Batt looked again at the sight in front of him and considered it actually not to be a wonder.

'I'm DI Batt,' he said.

'Yeh, I know who you are. And no, I didn't see anything.'

'Or hear anything?'

'What, with her downstairs with her telly on full blast all the time? It's a wonder I ain't deaf. Like her,' she added.

11

She looked at her watch and made to move off.
'Did you ever speak to him?'
'No. Don't even know his name.'
'Many visitors?'
'None that I ever saw.'
'So he kept himself to himself?'
'Suppose so. Look, I'm going to be late for …'
'The bingo. Which hall is it? The one that's just opened in Barr Gates?'
She nodded.
'Come on. I'll give you a lift. It's on my way back to the Station. Can't have you late. No blue lights, though.'

They moved off down the stairs just as the paramedics started to bring the body out.

Back outside in the sun the crowd was still waiting, growing impatient for a chance to see the final act of the drama before they got on with whatever they were planning to do before the inconvenience of someone's death had delayed them.

'Car's just round the corner. Sorry but I didn't catch your name.'
'That's because I didn't tell you.'

Batt turned to look at the woman who by now was red in the face and finding it hard to keep up with him.

'If you'd rather walk to the bingo that's up to you, but it would be helpful to have a name to go with your face,' he smiled.

'Elsie. Elsie Goodbody.'

Batt hid his grin. 'A misnomer living in a misnomer,' he thought.

'And I don't want no tv people coming round pestering me for being a witness either,' she continued. 'Least not till I've had me hair done on Monday.'

'Oh I'm sure we can see to that Mrs Goodbody.'

They reached the car and Batt unlocked. Mrs Goodbody heaved her perspiring body in and slammed the door. Batt went round to his side and started the engine.

'Seat belt on, Mrs Goodbody.'

He waited for her to finish wrestling with it and set off.

'Tell me, do you have many wins on the bingo?'

'This one has only just opened but I won ten pounds there last week. The other one I go to in Station Street has been there for years. I've had a few wins in my time.'

They joined the traffic on the main road into the town. As usual it was slow going.

'What's the biggest win you've had?'

'A few years back I won two hundred and fifty. That's me best but I've had my fair share of tens and twenties.'

'What do you spend it on?'

'Huh. It's spent before I get it. Rent's gone up, the kids are always needing new clothes and I'm still paying off the telly and the mobiles. I'm not looking forward to this winter I can tell you. The electric's bad enough in the summer. I had to borrow money to pay the bills last year and then borrow more money to pay this loan shark back.'

'You shouldn't go near loan sharks Mrs Goodbody.'

'I know that. We all of us know that but we can hardly go to the bank and ask them to lend us a few quid. "Mrs Goodbody, we need to know you can afford the repayments. Your account is already in the red. Do you have a fairy godmother who will help you out? No? Then you'll just have to beg a loan shark to see you right". Come on Mr Batt, get real It's loan sharks or freeze and starve.'

He couldn't think of a suitable reply so changed the subject.

'How many children do you have?'

'What is this? The Spanish Inquisition? Two. Jade's five and Billy's eight. They should be at school but it's closed today. Look, you can drop me here. It'll save you having to turn down Bethel Place. You'll never get out again with this traffic.'

Batt pulled in at the side of the road and Mrs Goodbody heaved herself out, a reverse operation to the way she'd got in.

'Thanks for the lift.'

He watched her – or more precisely he watched her voluminous pink shorts – disappear round the corner. What it brought to Batt's mind was Billy Connolly's "Hungry Bum Syndrome" and his explanation that "It's where your bum eats everything in its way. Chomp, chomp, chomp. You take your clothes off and there's no underwear there. Your bum has eaten it. You have to retrieve it with a crochet needle".

Chapter 2

Batt arrived back at the Station to a commotion at the sergeant's desk. A man was kicking off, venting his anger on anyone who cared to listen.

'I enna hophomonic,' he was saying. 'Am I hophomonic? I diddna do nothing wrong.'

Just at that moment he caught sight of Batt trying to go unnoticed down the corridor.

'Hey, Mr Batt,' he shouted, 'will youse tell 'em I ain't hossophomic.'

Batt sighed and walked back to the man who by now was having his shoes and belt removed.

'Mr Batt,' said the man, grimly holding on to his trousers to stop them from descending to the level of his pink Barbie socks, 'What have I done? I didnae do nothing.'

'Hello Tommy. Been celebrating again?'

'Aye what if I have? It was young Goatee's birthday. We was teaching him tae dance.'

'What's he supposed to have done, Sergeant?'

The sergeant looked down at the charge sheet.

'Drunk and disorderly outside Waitrose, and a complaint from a member of the public that he was shouting homophobic threats.'

'Well, Thomas. What do you have to say for yourself?' asked Batt whilst giving the arresting officer a wink.

'I told ye. We was teaching Goatee some proper dancing. The Gay Gordons. I shouted to him "Let's do the Gay Gordons" and the next thing I know is some woman has filmed us on her phone and called the police! What have I done wrong Mr Batt?'

'And this is just the start,' thought Batt.

'Just co-operate, Tommy, there's a good lad,' he said. 'We'll sort it later. They do a nice scrambled egg for lunch. You might still be in time if the sergeant here gets hold of the canteen and sweet-talks the cook.'

As the mollified customer was led away, still clutching his trousers to his waist, Batt called over the relieved arresting officer. 'Ye gods,' he thought, 'I must be getting old. The police are looking younger.'

'How old are you son?'

'Twenty-six, Sir.'

'And have you ever been to a barn dance?'

'A what, Sir?'

'A barn dance – where everyone wears cowboy outfits and sits on bales of hay drinking cider in some village hall.'

The young officer eyed him warily.

'You know, then they all stand up, hold hands and dance in a circle and swap partners.'

The wary look turned to one of alarm.

Batt ploughed on. 'One of the dances is called the Gay Gordons. When Tommy said they were all going to do the Gay Gordons he didn't mean they were going to do over a gay named Gordon.'

The officer stared uncomprehendingly at him.

'Look, just give him his scrambled egg, charge him with a disturbance of the peace, and release him. And for goodness' sake don't forget to give him his belt back or the next thing you know is someone will be complaining he's exposed himself in front of their terrified whippet.'

Before going to brief his team Batt made a call to Lucy, the "Burton Star" journalist who had been at Fairview Mansions. He found the relationship with the local Press to be symbiotic. They were able to find out things that people were reluctant to speak to the police about and, in return for tip-offs, Batt often gave them a helping hand with an article or two.

'DI Batt? What have you got for me?'

'First of all, Lucy, nothing attributable. The vic was a white male, probably in his sixties. Cause of death is as yet unknown but I can tell you it will be classified as suspicious. Possibly been dead for a day or two. Seems he was a bit of a loner. Neighbours thought he liked his drink. We'll be doing the usual door-to-door but you know what it's like for us – neighbours are reluctant to talk in case they end up on the wrong side of the gangs. If you hear anything useful you will let me know won't you?'

'Of course.'

There was a pause and then, 'So the XXL flamingo who accompanied you to your car isn't a suspect, then?'

Batt smiled to himself.

'No Lucy. I was helping her with a matter of greater importance than life and death. She was late for her morning fix of prize bingo down at that new place. "Eyesdown", isn't it called?'

'Yes. Big cash prizes, apparently. Thanks for phoning. Keep in touch.'

Batt promised he would and ended the call.

Major Incident Room Two was down the corridor from Batt's office. He could hear a buzz of conversation as he approached, punctuated by the occasional burst of laughter. He stood outside for a moment enjoying the sunshine that had defied the grime on the only window on that level, before turning through the door and into the gloom. The four officers present stood up when he entered and looked expectantly in his direction.

'Make yourselves comfortable,' said Batt. 'Probable homicide at Fairview Mansions on the Derby Road. I say 'probable' on the assumption the victim couldn't shoot himself in the head and then dispose of the weapon. Name on his driving licence is Kieran Wells. Apart from that, MIT's goody bag didn't have anything else in it apart from his watch and a few notes You're going to be spending the rest of the shift doing meet and greet with the neighbours.'

There was an air of resignation. Meet and greet was standard practice and hardly ever came up with anything useful. An elderly neighbour who thought she might have heard raised voices – but then again it could have been a tv - and an overweight middle-aged man on the sick who probably didn't know what day of the week it was and could they lend him a fiver until his unemployment payment came through so he could buy a few cans.

'Oh, and Helen, across the landing from the vic is a Mrs Goodbody. See if you can get her to go with you to Citizens Advice will you? She's got money problems and owes some loan shark or other. It's her two kids I'm worried about. They'll all be out on the street before you know it.

Now remember TIE. Trace, interview, eliminate. I want everyone in that block of flats interviewed. First a few things you should know. Let's hear what our fast-track grad has observed.'

All eyes turned to Talbot . For a moment he looked surprised but then gathered himself.

'Well,' he began, 'the victim was a white male, probably in his sixties or seventies. In need of a haircut and a shave. He had been shot in the head but for some reason there wasn't much blood. He obviously liked a drink because there were empty cans all over the place.'

Batt nodded at Talbot to continue.

'There's not much more I can add Sir.'

'Something for one of you to establish,' said Batt. 'Is there any CCTV footage, either inside or outside the building? James, could you take care of that?'

'One other thing I found strange.'

'Go on, Chris,' said Batt.

'There was nothing personal in the room. No photos or knicknacks.'

'Good point. Baz. Could you make a note of the driving licence details and run it past DVLA. Find the car and have it brought in for examination. If it's got a sat nav have the techies find out where it's been to in the past fortnight.'

Baz raised a hand in acknowledgement.

Finally he turned to Helen. 'Background checks please Helen – national insurance, bank accounts, mobile phone log; you know the drill. Start with a PNC search and go from there.

Right, let's see if we can impress the new Chief. Meet back here 0800 tomorrow for a debrief.' And seeing the looks of dismay added, 'I'll buy breakfasts. And you can use my coffee machine.'

The room cleared and Batt was left to his thoughts.

He'd not long been back at his desk with a fresh cup of coffee when his phone rang.

'DI Batt,' he said between sips.

A voice sounding remarkably similar to that of Margaret Thatcher greeted him. It was difficult to tell whether it belonged to a male or female.

'Detective Inspector. I'm the new Chief. I would like to see you in my office. Now!' the voice added before he could protest.

'Another wasted cup,' sighed Batt. It really was turning out to be a waste of money buying himself that coffee machine. Then he had second thoughts and decided to take his drink with him.

Climbing the stairs to the top floor, he stopped outside the Chief's office to get his breath back. He hoped the next bleep test wasn't due just yet; he needed to get back in shape. He took a sip and contemplated his lousy physical shape. Back in the day – and it was not really all that long ago – he could tab fifteen or twenty klicks in just over an hour. Things had started to go downhill with the death three years ago of Frances. It was a blow from which he still hadn't recovered.

He drained the cardboard cup and left it on a nearby radiator. He was about to open the door when his eyes were drawn to the new brass plaque with 'Ms P. Foster-Goode, Chief Constable' engraved on it. Also new were a couple of led lights, red and green, the red being illuminated. He knocked and, without waiting for a change of traffic light, entered.

The first thing he noticed were the two crossed hockey sticks hung on the wall facing him. Beneath them was an impressively large rosewood desk at which was seated a rather dumpy woman in a grey suit looking up at him. The power dressing was completed by a pair of shiny red shoes which glared threateningly at him from beneath the desk.

He decided he wasn't going to like her. It wasn't that he was sexist. He would have felt the same had it been a man wearing the shoes. But then he considered that, on reflection, perhaps he wouldn't have felt the same. He realised he was smiling.

'Something amusing you Detective Inspector?'

'No Ma'am. I just enjoy my work.'

She couldn't decide whether he was being sincere or showing a lack of respect for his senior officers that she'd been warned about. She decided it was the latter

'Did you not see the red light was on, Detective Inspector?'

'Sorry Ma'am. Must have missed it.'

She looked at him over her glasses.

'Do take a seat Batts,' she said.

'It's "Batt", Ma'am. There's only the one of me.'

'Now as you will be well aware this force has just failed its inspection on three counts. One: we have too few ethnic officers. Two: our statistical returns to the Home Office are overdue. Three: there have been too few prosecutions for hate crimes. You and your team will be tasked with improving our record on the latter.'

'But Ma'am..'

She looked up.

'We have a gunman on the loose and he – or she - needs bringing in before someone else dies.'

'Quite,' said his Chief Inspector. That's why, after you've attended the mortuary for the autopsy as Chief Investigating Officer, you will hand over the case to DI Mills. He may be young but he has impressed me with his grasp of procedure. Take DC Talbot along as the Exhibits Officer.'

'Ma'am I really think…' but she held up an imperial hand to silence further protest.

'I hear what you're saying, Batts, but hate crimes are your priority. And anyway I understand your methods of investigation are – how shall I put it – not appropriate to modern policing. Now, if you'll excuse me I have a Press conference to give.'

DI Mills was competent enough but something told Batt he didn't have the right background to get very far with this case. But he knew someone who did. If he was quick he would just about have time to see the Chief Super before dropping in on his Chief Constable's Press conference.

He walked down a flight of stairs to the level below and stopped outside Pete Jones's door. He knocked and waited until the door was opened by a tall athletic man of about Batt's age.

'George. I've been expecting you. Not happy with our new Chief Constable? Or are you out of coffee pods again?'

'Both,' said Batt. 'But the pods can wait.'

'Come in and make yourself comfy. Coffee? Decaff with a little milk, right?'

He moved across the room to where a kettle had recently boiled and took a couple of mugs from a cupboard. The kettle was switched on again.

'Now before you start, George, the Police Standards Commissioner has brought in the new Chief to raise standards. We're apparently failing to tick enough boxes. We're 'failing',' and here he used his fingers to imitate quotation marks, 'on three counts. One of them being prosecutions for hate crimes. I understand you've just been pulled off the Derby Road case and that your team has been assigned to dealing with the huge number of hate crimes that the Chief's TV appearance will be bound to generate.'

'With all due respect Pete, our new Chief Constable is too glitzy. And I bet she uses phrases like 'moving forwards' and 'drilling down'.'

'Nothing wrong with a bit of management speak."

He grinned. 'And with equal due respect George I agree with you. But if she can get the appropriate boxes ticked then the Force will no longer be classed as failing, the Commissioner will be re-elected on the strength of it, the Chief Inspector will be promoted to somewhere where she will be harmless and we all live happily ever after – in particular you with your clocks and me with the wife and the Triumph Stag. It's no time to kick up a fuss, George. It's not worth it.'

He poured water into the mugs and looked at Batt.

'You don't seem convinced. Look George, I know your record for solving serious crime. It's legendary round here. But I also know how you got some of those results. Let's just say the world has moved on from dinosaurs like ourselves. You and I go back a long way. Your intel saved lives in Afghanistan – more than once, come to think about it. When we left the army I climbed the greasy pole in the Force and now the most productive thing I do is get rid of coffee stains from this desk. You, on the other hand, chose to stay at the chalk face and solve crimes. But you lay a finger on a suspect these days and he'll have caught you on his phone and uploaded it to some cloud or other for the whole world to see before you can say "You're nicked"

Just go with the flow, George and don't rock the boat – for either of us.'

He passed Batt the mug. 'Chocolate biscuit?'

'The thing is, Pete, there's something about this Fairview Mansions murder that makes me think our military backgrounds might help.'

'Oh? In what way?'

'I'll know whether my suspicions are right or not when Siabhan does the autopsy tomorrow.'

He took a sip from his mug and replaced it on the desk.

'But this John Doe appears to have led two lives. He made out he was an alco to anyone coming to his door and yet the bedroom and bathroom were spotless. There was nothing to connect him to his past – no photos or anything else personal. The clothes were clean and ironed and arranged perfectly in the drawers.'

'OCD?'

'Could have been except for one thing. The bed had sheets, not a duvet. It was made the way we were taught in the army.'

'So what are you thinking?'

'He was in hiding from someone. As I say, I'll know more tomorrow.'

His superior looked thoughtfully at him.

'Has our vic got a name?'

'Kieran Wells,' replied Batt., 'according to his driving licence.'

'I'll see what I can do. But no promises, George. Now let's go and see what the new Chief has to say to the Press.'

They arrived and took their place at the back of the Press room just as Ms. Paula Foster-Goode was taking the stage. There were perhaps a dozen representatives from the media, dotted around the tiered seating. Batt recognised the reporter from the local radio station, and a couple of journalists from local newspapers. He assumed the others were from the ever increasing number of social media sites. "Click-baiters" the professionals called them. There was a moment's activity as coffee cups were placed on the floor and recording devices set up.

The new chief walked confidently across the raised platform and lowered herself onto a seat behind a long oak table. She was flanked by a couple of senior officers. Her red shoes were visible beneath it and seemed to Batt to be pointing directly at him. Had it been a James Bond film, he mused, they would probably have been able to shoot at him. She waited until the room was settled before introducing herself, but not, he noticed, the other two.

Her performance began with an explanation about her mission to improve upon certain aspects of the Force's performance, as identified by the latest inspection. She took a sip of water and surveyed those present in the room before launching into a lengthy diatribe against hate crimes.

'We need a society that is respectful of one another,' she concluded. 'This will be reflected in the way my officers deal with the public. I am urging anyone who feels they have been unfairly treated to come forward and make a complaint. In the same way, anyone who feels a member of the public has been offensive towards their gender, sexual orientation, age, race or physical appearance should also file a complaint. Now, I'm happy to take some questions from the floor.'

There was a somewhat stunned silence before someone raised their hand, introduced themselves and asked whether she could confirm there had been a murder at Fairview Mansions and if so what was known so far.

Batt's new Chief looked a little taken aback that the question was not related to her topic, but explained that, yes, there had been an incident involving a male, believed to have been in his sixties, which the police were treating as a suspicious death.

Another questioner asked how the enquiry was progressing. Ms. Foster-Goode looked in the direction of one of her two senior officers who explained that the police were continuing with their enquiries and were following up several leads.

'Has the deceased been named?'

'We are withholding that until next of kin have been contacted.'

'Is it drugs related?'

'It is too early to make any links.'

The room fell silent. It was obvious the police were not going to comment further. The reporters retrieved their coffee cups and began to pack away their things. The Chief exited stage left and it was one of the senior officers who thanked everyone for coming.

Batt and Pete were about to leave when their way was barred by an excited young reporter.

'Jenny Beamish from Burton Spotted. Look, I just have to know. Were they Jimmy Choo shoes Ms. Foster-Goode was wearing?'

The two men exchanged looks before Batt replied that no, as far as he knew they were her own.

'Do you even know who Jimmy Choo is?' asked Pete after she'd stalked off.

'No idea. And if those really were his shoes then I'd rather not know in case I'm accused of questioning his sexual orientation.'

They made their way back upstairs to Jones's office.

'Come on George. Let's have another brew. When all these hate crime complaints start flooding in you won't have time to eat let alone drink. And I'm sorry about your team being landed with the job. I tried my best to talk the Chief out of it but she insisted it would be good for your – and I quote - "ongoing self awareness development".'

Batt sat himself down and watched as Jones set the coffee machine going. He couldn't help but notice it was a much superior model to his own rather basic one.

'I think I got enough in the way of ongoing self awareness development when we were dealing with the Taliban twenty odd years ago. Anyway, how's the family? I seem to remember you were telling me your eldest lad was thinking of university?'

'Ben? No, he's been there, done that, got the hangover. He finished three years ago.'

Batt took the cup he was offered. And the coaster.

'Started work at an undertaker's.'

'Don't tell me you need a degree to bury people now.'

'Wouldn't be surprised but no, he's in their accounts department. It's Dan who's thinking of uni. He's been put off by the size of Ben's student loan. As he says, it's bigger than the amount you'd need for a deposit on a house. No wonder kids are still living with their parents until their mid thirties.'

'True. Look, Pete, getting back to the Fairview case. If the dead man really is ex-military then don't you think we owe him a thorough investigation?'

Jones finished the last of his coffee and held the mug in his hands whilst he thought things over.

'You're right of course, but at the moment it's only an if. Then there's the question of how we get around Ms. Foster-Goode's decision to put young Millsie in charge of the case.'

He put the mug down on his desk and came to a decision.

'Look, let's wait for the autopsy report. If there's anything that points to him being ex-army then I'll try and pull a few strings. Who is the pathologist, by the way?'

'Siobhan.'

'Good. Let me know when she's got some results and we'll take it from there.'

Batt thanked him for the drink and made his way back downstairs.

Blue team were not best pleased when told they had been moved from the suspected murder case to dealing with hate crime complaints. They had clearly been looking forward to doing some real detective work.

They stopped talking and turned to Batt as he entered.

The looks on their faces told him news had already reached them.

'How did you find out?' he asked.

'We were in the canteen,' said Helen. 'DI Mills and his lot came bursting in like excited school kids. They couldn't wait to tell us.'

'Yes, well, you're disappointed. I'm disappointed. But the lady is not for turning, it seems.

I blame myself, of course. If only I hadn't beaten a confession out of that elderly lady who had parked her mobility scooter on double yellows.'

Baz added,'It wasn't just that, Sir. It was when you had the scooter seized and sent to the crusher.'

Helen saw the look on Chris's face as he stared at his Inspector.

'They're joking, Chris.'

'Our new Chief, Ms. P. Foster-Goode...'

'She of the red shoes,' interrupted Baz.

'Good observational skills, Baz. Yes, she of the red shoes has decided that putting us on hate-crime watch will be good for my ongoing self awareness situation. Her words, not mine

So whilst DI Mills and his gang are out enjoying the sunny weather we'll be confined to this architectural gem listening to Jo Public auditioning for the Jeremy Kyle Show.'

He moved across to his desk and glanced out of the window which looked down on the Station's car park.

DI Mills had clearly not wasted any time. Batt watched him striding purposefully over to where the pool cars were parked, his merry band in tow. He said a few words to them before they got into a couple of Volvo estates and drove off through the gates to join the queue of vehicles leaving the town. Batt couldn't help but notice that Mills had somehow managed to bag the newest of the Force's fleet.

Batt sighed and turned round to face his team.

'Look, the best thing we can do is be professional about this. Amongst the time wasters will be some genuine cases that need our attention.'

He reached for his phone and got through to admin.

'Hi Twinkletoes, it's DI Batt. If you get any hate crime files can you bring them over to my office please?'

He listened for a moment, laughed, and said,' Yes, I've upset her already.'

Chapter 3

The next morning saw Batt looking mournfully at the growing pile of folders on his desk. The door opened and Talbot walked in. Batt looked round.

'For God's sake, Chris.'

'Sir?'

'You know they call me "Batt Man" and in you come wearing a bright red shirt.'

'Sir?'

Annette from admin tapped on the door, entered, said 'Hi Robin, like the shirt' and without breaking step placed another folder on the desk.

'Look at this lot, DC Talbot. They're all isms.'

'Sir?'

'Isms. You know, sexism, racism, ageism … And what's this one you've just brought me, Twinkle Toes?'

'Apparently Sir it's from a student. Complaint that his lecturer insists on calling him "he" whereas he wants to be addressed as "they".'

Batt's eyes bulged. 'What is he? A schizophrenic? "They" is plural – more than one. Does he think there is more than one of him? The singular is "it". He should be called "It" if he insists on being gender neutral.'

Annette smiled at him and exited stage left, the sound of her heels growing fainter in the silence that followed.

The day had started well enough. Although forensics had established nothing to link the body to the wardrobe, the car had been found late afternoon not far from the flat. It did indeed have a sat nav which had recorded several local journeys and one in particular that had had Batt's nose twitching: Hereford.

He returned to the present. He was down the cost of four breakfasts but only one hate-crime folder.

'It's those idiot politicians that I blame, Chris. They see a vote catcher and before you can count to ten the police have been tasked with enforcing it with the threat of being labelled "failing" if they don't. How many officers are going to be tied up wasting their time establishing whether Gerald was dismissed from his call-centre job because he was old or because – most likely – he was simply useless.'

At this point Batt's composure broke completely and in one sudden movement of his right hand swiped the folders off his desk and scattered them all over the floor. They were both staring down at them in surprise when the phone rang.

'Yes, Ma'am,' he said, 'DC Talbot and I are looking at them now.'

They managed to suppress their laughter just long enough for Batt to put the phone back in its cradle.

'Right, come on Chris, better make a start before Dr Fahy phones about the autopsy. What's the one nearest to you?'

Talbot bent down and opened the file.

'Sir, it's a complaint from someone who said, and I quote, Sir, "Some Welsh git called me a Scottish laird".'

'Do we have the name of the complainant?'

"A Mr. Duncan Macduff."

'Oh for Pete's sake. And does Mr Macduff know what a laird is?'

'Apparently not Sir. He just assumed it was something offensive.'

He read on and added, 'The interviewing officer thinks the accused was probably just trying to be friendly on account of his name being the same as a Scottish laird in "Macbeth". It's a play by Shakespeare, Sir...'

'I know who Macduff was, Talbot! Send an armed rapid response team to the man's address, have him brought in and held for questioning.'

'Sir?' said Talbot, looking shocked.

'I'm joking,' growled Batt.

His DC gestured to another folder.

'Yes, pick it up. Let's see if this one will get the Chief Constable any brownie points.'

It was at that moment the phone rang again.

'Be with you in twenty minutes,' Batt said after a brief pause. 'Come on Chris. Proper work to do. Autopsy to attend.'

The drive through Burton was the usual slow crawl, made worse by several sets of temporary traffic lights. Apart from the odd idle JCB digger there was nothing to suggest work was about to start any time soon. Finally he swung the Mondeo into the mortuary car park and undid his seat belt. Talbot followed suit and soon they were walking up the steps of a single storey building and entering a spartan waiting room. Batt pressed an intercom button and announced himself and Talbot. He heard the click of a door unlocking and a figure dressed in green scrubs and a mask emerged.

'Hi George, Chris. Come through and get yourselves kitted out.'

They followed her through to a changing area and put on plastic coveralls and hairnets.

'Here Chris,' said Batt reaching into his pocket and pulling out a jar of Vic. 'This your first post mortem?'

'Sir,' said Talbot.

'If you think you're going to faint then come and sit in here for a bit. Nothing to be ashamed of. It can come as a bit of a shock if you're not expecting it.'

Siabhan Fahy smiled. 'You've not seen our new toy then George? Follow me. Hopefully I'll not need to unzip the body.'

She led the way down the corridor and through a set of doors.

'The body's been washed and the attendants have sent the body bag off to forensics. Not that I think we'll learn anything from it.'

On the other side of the door they were met by a glass partition in front of which was a console with a large monitor screen at which sat a technician in a white lab coat. On the other side of the glass was a large white tube with what looked like a conveyor belt leading into it.

'It's a scanner,' said Batt.

'Correct,' confirmed Siobhan. " A VA table to be precise. It will take about three minutes to do a top-to-toe scan. It will show three planes as it goes down the body. We'll be able to look at the condition of vital organs such as the heart and the liver. Then we'll do a metal tracker to see if there are any metal fragments.'

As she was speaking two porters wheeled in a gurney and lifted a body from it and onto the conveyor belt. Siobhan gave the technician the go-ahead to begin, the lights dimmed and the body slowly disappeared into the tunnel. A few minutes later the clanking noises stopped and the body reappeared.

'We'll do a quick assessment of the vital organs and then start the metal tracker.'

Siobhan and the technician studied the scans on the computer screen whilst Batt and Talbot looked on.

'Everything looks normal, George. No enlargement of the heart, kidneys look normal and the liver is in a healthy state – so no excessive alcohol consumption.'

She turned to the technician. 'Metal tracker?'

The body began to move into the tunnel again and almost immediately a buzzer sounded.

'Metal fillings in the teeth. We'll do a test on them later.'

The body continued on its way until the buzzer sounded again just before the legs disappeared. Its progress was paused.

'Bit young for a hip replacement. Let's enlarge to a 3D image, please.'

The technician pressed a key on the keyboard and an image filled the screen.

'There are fragments of metal in the lower abdomen, George. When we've done here we'll go back to the morgue and I'll open him up.'

The rest of the scan continued without interruption.

The lights went up again and Siobhan turned to Batt and Talbot.

'The porters will take the body back. We might as well have a cup of tea whilst we wait for them. Mike,' she said to the technician, ' thanks for that. Will you go over the scans again in case I've missed anything? And can you send the pictures through to my computer, please?'

She stood up and stretched. 'I'll be sending the images to a couple of other pathologists to check I haven't missed anything. Follow me gents. I might even find a biscuit to go with the tea.'

Twenty minutes later Batt and Talbot found themselves looking across a large white-tiled room . The glare of numerous strip lights did little to improve the cold atmosphere. There were what looked like large filing cabinets down two sides and towards the centre several stainless steel tables with banks of lights above them – the sort you looked up at from a dentist's chair. On one of them was the Fairview Mansions victim.

Batt took out his jar of Vic again and dabbed some under his nose. He offered the pot to Talbot who did the same. The smell of formalin was overpowering.

Siobhan rinsed her hands at a sink before replacing her mask and beckoning them over.

'Ready?' she asked. She switched on a dictaphone and began a commentary.

'Let's begin with an external examination. Date: 8th September 2024. Time: 10:15am. Present is Dr Siobhan

Fahy, pathologist, DI George Batt the Crime Scene Manager, and DC Chris Talbot who is acting as Exhibits Manager. We have the body of a white male, aged approximately seventy years, who was discovered deceased on the morning of 6th September in his apartment at Fairview Mansions on the Derby Road in Burton on Trent.'

She pulled back the sheet to uncover the head. 'There is a gunshot wound to the forehead. The weapon appears to have been discharged from fairly close range judging by the scorch marks around the entry.'

The examination continued for over an hour, with surprising results: The victim had had dental work done that was not typically British; he had had facial reconstruction; there was evidence of scarring on the arms from the removal of tattoos.

'Let's have a look for that metal in the abdomen,' said Siobhan, picking up a scalpel from a tray of surgical instruments. She began to make an incision about six centimetres in length just above the naval. The flesh split open.

Batt looked across at Talbot who gave him a nod and the thumbs up sign.

Siobhan put her hand into the opening and rooted around. When the hand emerged it held a few pieces of bloodied flesh and some small fragments of metal.

'Shrapnel?' asked Batt.

'Could be. I'll have the lab do some tests. I'll also have them do some fluids tests.'

She placed the contents into a steel tray.

'While I've got him opened up, let's see if the stomach contents can tell us what he ate last.'

She picked up the scalpel and set to work.

'Looks like some kind of cereal – probably muesli which suggests he met his end sometime in the morning. Any muesli in his flat?'

'I'll have it checked,' said Batt.
'If there is then we can see if there's a match.'
She switched off her dictaphone, and began to sew the incisions up. When all was done she peeled off her latex gloves.

'Could be a couple of days before I can give an accurate time of death, and a bit longer before we have the results of a toxicology report. I'll also have the metal fragments analysed. I'll inform the coroner.

I'll tell you one thing, George. However he died it wasn't from a gun shot wound. Hardly any loss of blood which suggests he was killed before he was shot. My guess is he was injected with something lethal in the chair in which his body was discovered. If the lab results show that to be the case I'll do a full body check for a puncture wound.'

Batt arrived back at the Station just in time for lunch. Chris Talbot had excused himself, saying he could do with some fresh air. The canteen was its usual busy self, most conversation seemingly given over to an appraisal of the Chief Constable's press conference. His team was seated at their usual table. He paid and took his tray of mackerel fillets and salad over to where they had made a space for him.

'Didn't fancy the meat pie?' asked James.

'James,' said Batt spearing a piece of tomato with his fork, 'you don't end up with a body for a temple by eating offal. And anyway it's the sticky toffee pudding I'll be having for afters.'

Baz asked how the Press conference had gone.

Batt explained that the Chief had rather taken the room by surprise by focusing on hate crimes and how the public should not hesitate to come forward if they felt they had been victims.

'They thought they were there to be briefed about the murder.'

' Was she asked about it?'

'Oh yes,' said Batt, removing a mackerel bone from between his front teeth. He placed it on the edge of his plate.

'So what did she have to say about it?' asked Helen.

'Just that the police were treating the death as suspicious and that her team were following several leads. Which was news to me. Unless,' he added, 'Millsie has had a sudden breakthrough since taking over the case an hour ago.'

As if on cue, DI Mills entered the canteen, followed by a couple of his disciples. He scanned the room for a spare table and caught sight of Batt.

'Ah, Batt Man, 'he called in a voice that could be heard even over the clattering of plates and the sudden hiss of the expresso coffee machine. 'You and Blue team just taxing your brains over a few name-calling cases? Chief clearly thinks you're up to it or she wouldn't have pulled your lot off the Fairview murder. Don't worry, though, the investigation is now in safe hands.'

Behind him his officers clearly thought their DI was a card.

Batt ignored him and turned back to his table.

'Helen, have you anything I can pass on to The Joker following your background investigations?'

'No Sir. Everything checks out. Tax, National Insurance, driving licence details, bank account. He paid his rent by direct debit from that account. His phone is with BT. I'm waiting for them to send details of his call log. By the way, Sir, was there a mobile phone with his personal effects?'

'Nothing handed over to me,' replied Batt, reaching for the salt. 'Why do you ask?'

'No landline at the flat, Sir. Oh, and I couldn't find any medical or dental records.'

'Not to worry. You've done well. Thanks Helen. Anyway, not our concern any more. Let DI Mills and his team claim the glittering prizes. We've got a few so-called hate crimes to investigate. I'll see you all back at the office in ten minutes.'

Just as they were clearing away their plates Baz asked how the autopsy had gone.

Batt gave a shrug of the shoulders.

'Need to wait for a few lab results,' he said non-committally, 'but quite interesting.''He was left picking bones out of his mackerel.

"In fact very interesting,' he thought to himself.

It was later that afternoon by the time Batt had had a chance to organise his team to read through the files that were now miraculously back on top of his desk He excused himself and went down to the front reception. Annette looked up from her work station and smiled.

'What can I do for you, Sir?'

'Annette, do you know where Superintendent James is at the moment?'

She looked surprised at the question, wondering why he hadn't tried to ring him from his office phone, but simply said, 'In his lair I think. Do you want me to phone and check?'

Batt nodded and waited, admiring the new posters that had appeared on the wall in reception. In bold red lettering *"We Hate Hate Crime"* read one whilst another showed a scene in which a crying Muslim girl was being laughed at by a group of teenage white youths. Underneath was the caption, *"This Is A Crime. Report It"*. Batt caught himself nodding in agreement.

Annette gave a gentle cough.

'He's in, Sir, and he will see you now if you'd like to go up.'

Batt nodded his thanks and set off up the nearest stairs, glancing round before knocking on Superintendent James' door.

'Well speak of the devil,' said Pete, indicating a seat opposite his desk. 'There's a fire extinguisher over by the window. You'll need one,' he continued, 'to put out the flames coming from your ears. Coffee?'

Batt nodded. 'No sugar…..'

'…just a pinch of salt,' laughed James.

'I bet with it being sunny you'd rather be ruining a good walk playing a round of golf than sitting in here.'

James got up out of his seat, walked over to a table in the corner and switched on the coffee machine.

'Anything's better than sitting by a river bank all day and catching nothing but a cold.'

'Touchee. Is that ex-Burton Albion player still a member? You know, the one that used to play for Derby? Can't think of his name.'

'Pete Styles? Yes he gets the odd round in. Knees are playing him up, though, so he hasn't been seen much lately. He reckons he played on for a couple of seasons too many.'

The coffee machine began to make spitting noises.

'Is it supposed to do that?' asked Batt.

'Lord knows. Haven't read the instructions. Seems to make decent coffee, though.'

He waited a moment before filling two cups and looking directly at Batt.

'I've some news for you. There's a pool car booked for Monday. Have a drive down to Hereford.'

Batt sat up suddenly in his seat, slopping coffee down his clean shirt. James took a tissue from a box on his desk and offered it.

'So you did have a word with Hereford. I was right, then.'

'I read your prelim report on the case. The sat nav destination to Hereford got me wondering.'

'This Kieran Wells was ex-army?'

'Yes... and no. You'll be told more when you get there, I expect. Just report to the guard room, give them your name, and they'll sort you out.'

Batt stood and put the stained tissue in the bin on his way to the door, wiping his fingers on the back of his trousers.

'Oh George.'

'Boss?'

'As far as anyone else is concerned you're just off to make routine hate crime enquiries. If Brown Owl comes sniffing I'll tell her you're following up on one of the complaints. And by the way, the car's sat nav has been disabled so either take a map book or make sure your phone is fully charged.'

****

Batt wiled away a peaceful weekend at his home in nearby Bishops Bromley. It was a pleasant enough village with its fair share of timbered buildings. At the centre was the village green with its Buttercross. He had read that the village – then described as a town – had been granted a royal charter in the fourteenth century to hold a weekly market under it. The place had flourished until the coming of the railways, when it became something of a backwater. The village was quite a tourist attraction: Mary Queen of Scots had had a comfort break just up the road, on her way to Warwick Castle, and Dick Turpin was supposed to have spent the night in one of the pubs on the day he had stolen Black Bess from the horse fair in a neighbouring town. Ben Johnson and his father would have passed through on their way from Lichfield to sell books at Uttoxeter. Perhaps Bishops Bromley's chief claim to fame was its annual Horn Dance. It dated back to medieval times and involved a team of men in costumes dancing round the parish from sunrise to sunset, carrying sets of reindeer antlers on their shoulders. They were accompanied by an accordian player and someone dressed up as Maid Marion whose chief task was to persuade the crowds of followers to part with their cash. By the time they danced outside Batt's house on the main street it was evening and the visits to the village's numerous public houses had taken their toll. He had found through experience that it was safest to hang out of his bedroom window and throw a few coins to Maid Marion. Get too close and you'd be beaten about the head by a pig's bladder.

He had two longcase clocks to work on, bought recently online from a Lichfield auction house. One in particular he was very pleased with – a brass faced eight day clock with a moonphase. It had been made in the 1750s by a local man from Uttoxeter. Batt always marvelled at the precision of the movements in these old clocks, especially considering the clock makers only had hand tools at their disposal. No 3D printers in those days.

He had the movement in pieces on the bench in his workshop. The door was open and he could hear the sounds of children in the playground of the nearby primary school. Saturday cricket, or maybe rounders.

He picked up the escape wheel and its arbor. These old clocks had remarkably little friction so that the only real wear was to the escapement. He attached the part to a machine and set it going. One of the teeth was out of true and the angles needed resetting. No big deal. He would immerse everything in an electrolyte bath first to clean the brass.

He collected up all the parts, placed them in the fluid and switched on. It would take two or three hours, during which time he would turn his attention to the oak and mahogany case. Some of the stringing was in need of repair and, as usual, the trunk door key was missing so he'd have to see if any of his collection of spares would fit.

He carried out a couple of trestles and positioned them on the slabs outside his workshop. He was just going back to fetch the clock case when he heard the sound of his gate latch. He looked down the garden and saw Jack walking towards him. Despite the heat he was dressed, as usual, in a heavy coat and cowboy hat.

'Jack, just the man. Can you do a bit of wood turning for me? One of the pillars on a clock hood needs replacing.'

'I can do that for you, ta very much, thank you. Have you been buying more clocks?'

'Just a couple. You know I can't resist. Come on into the kitchen where it's cooler. You must be hot in that coat. Fancy a cold drink?'

'Yes, thank you,' came the slowly-spoken reply. 'Thank you very much, ta thank you.'

'Any shopping I can do for you? I'm off to Uttoxeter this afternoon.'

'I'm alright, thank you. Sarah across the road went yesterday to get me a few bits. I've started to have these ready meals you know, now that I'm on my own.'

His eyes started to brim.

'They're all right, you know. I don't feel much like cooking any more, now that….'

Batt handed him a glass of elderflower juice.

'What have you got planned for tomorrow?'

'Nothing really, thank you.'

'How about I pack up a few bits to eat and we'll have an afternoon's fishing down at the reservoir?'

'That's really kind of you George. I'd like that, thank you very much. I haven't been fishing in ages.'

'If you catch anything, you're cooking tea.'

'Aye, right you are.'

'How are your tubs? Hope you've been watering them.'

Batt was opening tins looking for some cake his neighbour had left by his back door a couple of days ago.

'I see you've got some geraniums planted.'

'I have. I went into Uttoxeter and bought three trays from the supermarket. I forgot I'd have to carry them home on the bus so I had to get a taxi. Guess how much.'

Batt finally located the cake and brought it over to the table.

'Five pounds?'

'Seven pounds eighty-five.'

'They turned out to be expensive plants then.'

'Aye they did that, George.'

He took the slice of sponge Batt offered him.

'How are you getting on with that new pacemaker?'

'Marvellous. Do you know they can adjust it remotely? I've to go back to Burton next week to have it checked. Not had another funny turn since it's been fitted.'

'If I'm free I'll take you. You don't want to have to rely on an ambulance. Getting there's OK but you could be waiting hours for one to bring you home.'

'That's very kind of you, ta thank you, but you're a busy man George so I'll book an ambulance.'

'Well the offer's always there,' said Batt. 'Can I top your glass up?'

'Thank you but I'd best be off. I've got them tubs to water. Let me know about that wood turning you want doing.'

With a final 'thank you, ta thank you,' he drained his glass, picked up his hat, and left.

Batt brought to mind the words of Dylan Thomas. "Time held me green and dying". It was true. Every passing day was a day closer to death. Perhaps for Jack it couldn't come soon enough. He'd lived in the village all his life and had married his childhood sweetheart. After almost sixty years of contentment she had died, leaving Jack on his own and unable to come to terms with the solitude and growing sense of desolation. Batt knew the feeling only too well. He looked across the kitchen to the photograph of his wife on the wall. How long was it now since Fran had died? He knew the answer without needing to think: three years and four months.

He wandered back outside and carried on working on his clocks.

'Though I sang in my chains like the sea'.

Batt walked slowly back down the path to his workshop. The church clock was striking five. He decided to spend another hour working on the clock before thinking about what to have for tea. He really ought to go on a run but it was still too hot. Perhaps later.

He carried the clock case out of the workshop and placed it on the trestles, and then went back in for a tin of Briwax. He had been polishing for a while when his mind turned to the murder of Kieran Wells.

Chapter 4

Monday morning saw Batt drop his bergen onto the front passenger seat of a Volvo estate and drive out of the police compound towards the A38. He waited until the lights changed by the National Museum of Brewing with its old steam locomotive on display. His father always said the children he taught were more compliant when there was the smell of hops in the air. The only time he dare try to teach them poetry. Well, the poetry the Head found acceptable, that is. Apparently he had once read Auden to them and next day had been hauled over the carpet following an avalanche of complaints from horrified parents. It was a poem about the way your parents messed up your life. Maybe the complaints were justified.

He turned right at the island near Burton Albion's Pirelli Stadium and on past the Pirelli warehouse.

The day had started bright and warm. He wasn't too impressed that he'd been given a car with a gear stick. His own car was an automatic. One thing he found himself agreeing with the Americans on – in fact probably the only thing – was how much of a no-brainer it was to drive a car that didn't trouble your left arm and left leg. Batt turned on the car's air con and then fiddled with the radio until he found a station playing music from the 1960s. Dusty was part way through "You Don't Have To Say You Love Me". Batt pictured her in a silver gown, arms stretched out in a dramatic pose.

He settled back in the Volvo's comfy seat and began to relax. He reckoned on a journey of about two hours.

The A38 was its usual busy self, the congestion made worse as he slowed to a crawl on the approach to the Lichfield slip road. There was a lane closure due to work on HS2. Batt thought the plans for the high speed rail link had been scrapped but looking down to his left at the acres of muddy wasteland and the huge dumper trucks racing across it suggested otherwise.

He wasn't what you'd call a tree hugger, but he had despaired when whole swathes of ancient woodland had disappeared at nearby Fradley. The ironic thing was that, now the plans had changed, thousands of saplings had been planted to replace the trees that had been cut down.

The traffic was now at a standstill. He sat looking at the rear of an HGV that had come from Poland and wondered whether they experienced the same sort of delays over there.

With a hiss of air brakes the lorry moved forward only to come to a halt again a few metres further on.

Batt glanced at the sat nav on his phone. He still had ample time to get to Hereford and his meeting.

He wondered who he would be seeing and what he would be told. Pete James hadn't wasted any time in getting hold of someone who knew the name "Kieran Wells". The cloak and dagger aspect was also interesting. Pete had gone behind the Chief Inspector's back in arranging this visit. He pictured little antennae twitching at the ends of the red shoes back at the Station and hoped his old CO wasn't putting his neck on the line.

The lorry inched forward again and this time kept moving, gradually increasing speed. Before long the lane closure ended and the traffic settled down again into its natural rhythm.

The radio station was now playing Roy Orbison singing "In Dreams".

He hoped this visit to Hereford wasn't going to end in a nightmare.

His estimate of two hours wasn't far off and he arrived at the Hereford Barrack's Stirling Lines gatehouse late morning.

The barracks themselves – several blocks or two and three storey red brick buildings - were laid out on a vast lawned campus interspersed with some immaculately kept borders of red, white and blue plants. The facility was protected by some wire mesh security fencing. Batt wondered how easy it would be to penetrate it. It certainly didn't look too difficult for someone with a pair of wire cutters. He waited in line behind a delivery lorry which was being thoroughly gone over by two soldiers, and studied the mass of surveillance cameras mounted on a pole. Eventually he was signalled to drive the Volvo between two tall brick pillars and towards the squat white gatehouse.

A guard appeared at the door and motioned him to lower his window. The hot air he was met with came as something of a shock after the cool of the air con. The guard disappeared inside again but after a few seconds reappeared and strode up to the car. Batt switched off the radio.

'Mr Batt. Good morning, sir. You are expected. Keep to the left and take the first turn on the right. Park up in front of the brick building with white rendering above the door. You will be met there.'

Batt thought the security checks on him were a little lax and said so.

'Oh I shouldn't worry detective. Let's just say your face is familiar to our surveillance cameras. In any case you've been escorted all the way from Burton. Just a training exercise. We often do covert exercises like this with members of the public. With you it was too good an opportunity to miss. A man of your background, I'm surprised you didn't spot us.'

'Blame Dusty,' said Batt, 'and a comfortable car. Keep left and take the first right?'

'Yes sir. And mind the sleeping policeman.'

Batt couldn't work out whether this was a dig at his powers of observation or a warning about grounding the car on some speed bumps.

He passed white painted finger signs for A,B,D and G squadrons and their 'T'-shaped buildings, before pulling up, as instructed, in front of a two-storey building that formed one side of a quadrangle. He made sure the lid was on his Costa Coffee cup before reaching for his jacket from the back seat. The heat hit him again as he opened the door. He stretched, listening to the familiar sound of square bashing going on somewhere over to his right, the parade ground's clock tower just visible between two blocks of buildings. *'We are the pilgrim's master. We shall go always a little further'* was inscribed around its base, Batt recalled.

For a moment he was back in the 1990s, remembering his first few days as a squaddie. It hadn't been Hereford then, though. It was only several years later that he had made the newly-completed SAS headquarters at Stirling Lines his home. The drone of a lawn mower's got louder and suddenly appeared from around the corner of the building. Batt had to smile: it was painted in desert camouflage colours.

'To be expected,' he thought. He waited for it to rattle past, exchanging waves with the operator and made his way along a gravelled path towards the building he had been directed to. Before he got too far the door opened and a female in civilian clothes came out to meet him. She smiled and asked him to follow her.

Once inside, it took Batt some time for his eyes to get used to the relative darkness of a large, panelled entrance hall. Looking around he could see it was quite some place. Regimental flags were on display around the walls, vases of flowers standing in niches between them. Photographs of past SAS members were everywhere , the largest and most prominent being that of Lieutenant Colonel David Stirling himself.

Batt was handed a folder.

'I've been asked to make sure you read this whilst you're waiting, Sir. You won't be kept long.'

He found himself a seat in a shaded part of the room and opened the file. It was Siobhan's report. He skimmed the first part, having been present when she explained the cosmetic surgery to the face, the foreign dental work and the removal of tattoos from the arms, and focussed his attention on the analysis of bodily fluids. There was no trace of alcohol or drugs in Wells's system. This did not particularly surprise him. What did make him sit up was the toxicology report. Siobhan had evidently had to seek the expertise of Professor Forrest at her old university in Sheffield before stating there was sodium pentothal in the blood. A hair analysis had confirmed it. Sodium pentothal, Batt knew, was a Russian made psychoactive drug – a truth drug which slowed metabolic activity in the brain, making it hard to lie. According to the lab report there was over 300mg per litre present in Wells's system. That would have been enough to kill a person. What was not in the report, however, was the analysis of the metal fragments found in the abdomen. It was most unlike Siobhan to overlook something.

He was still thinking over the implications when the woman returned and collected the folder.

There were numerous unmarked doors leading off the entrance hall and Batt was led through one and down a corridor. Through the windows he could see the mower man was cutting perfect stripes as he thrummed up and down the lawn. He hurried to catch up with the woman and joined her just as she was tapping a code into an electronic lock. She stood aside and let him enter, the door closing softly behind him.

Across the far side of the room sat a man behind a large oak desk. He was older than Batt had expected – mid sixties he would have guessed. He was casually dressed in cream trousers and denim shirt and clearly kept himself in trim. The man rose and held out his hand. Batt shook it, noticing the little finger was missing.

'DI Batt. Welcome to the inner sanctum. Please take a seat. My name is O'Brien. As in Orwell's "Nineteen Eighty Four".'

'So what have you found my worst fear is, Mr O'Brien, for when you put me in Room 101?'

'Not rats,' said O'Brien. 'I would say hate-crime files.'

Batt looked surprised for a moment before nodding.

'I work for MI5's Force Research Unit,' continued O'Brien sitting himself down again, 'which, as you know, does not officially exist, even though our Bessbrook base in South Armagh is hardly a secret. A Google search probably lists our phone number. Anyway no doubt you've heard rumours about us from your days in Afghanistan. Before we get to discussing Kieran Wells I want you to sign this.'

He took a sheet of paper from a drawer and placed it where Batt could read it.

'It's a copy of the Official Secrets Act. I signed up for that years ago,' replied Batt.

'Not this version,' he was told. 'This one is for advanced operations. If you break it we will shoot you.'

Batt couldn't decide whether the man was being serious or not. He suspected he probably was. O'Brien handed him a pen. Batt considered for a moment or two and then added his signature. Whatever this man had in mind for him it had to be better than sifting through endless folders of alleged hate crimes.

'Let's have a little chat over coffee and then we can get some lunch.'

He picked up the phone and ordered coffee and biscuits, then drummed his fingers on the desk top as if wondering where to begin. He caught sight of Batt looking at his hand.

'The finger? Missing in action. It's probably still where I left it in County Tyrone. And speaking of Northern Ireland, as you will be aware the Northern Ireland Assembly has just reconvened. A Sinn Fein minister is leading it. For them that's something of a breakthrough and they don't want anyone rocking the boat. There are now more Catholics in the north than Protestants, and Sinn Fein hopes that, with a bit of tinkering with constituency boundaries, it won't be long before they have a democratically elected majority.'

Batt considered the implications of this before asking, 'But how will they be able to become part of Ireland now we are out of Europe? Surely the British government would never hand the north over? OK so Wales and Scotland have been allowed to go their own ways to an extent, but they are still part of the UK. I mean, look at the Scottish parliament's attempt to introduce new laws about gender. The UK government soon declared it wasn't lawful and pulled the rug from under their feet. And defence-wise we're still all part of a United Kingdom.'

'There was always a desire amongst Sinn Fein's leaders to take control of the north. The last thing they wanted was to give their hard-earned power away to Ireland's politicians. Yes it was convenient to have the Irish government believe in a united Ireland because it gave the IRA a safe house for its operations. The likes of Martin McGuiness and Gerry Adams are power hungry. As I say, they and their pals don't want anything getting in the way now they feel their goal is within sight.'

'You say they don't want any trouble. What sort of trouble?'

'There are plenty of ex combatants on all sides – Republicans, Unionists, RUC and British Army – who feel they have old scores to settle. They're knocking on a bit, most of them, and their time is running out. At the moment any score-settling has been under control. All sides recognise the advantage of keeping the status quo but it only takes one individual to break ranks and all hell will break loose in the way of reprisals. We'll be back to where we started when the Troubles began in the Seventies.'

The door clicked open and a squaddie carrying a tray entered. O'Brien gestured for him to place it on the desk which he did before saluting smartly and disappearing.

'I believe you take it with a pinch of salt?'

For the second time in a matter of minutes Batt looked surprised.

'So where does Kieran Wells come in to this?'

Batt was handed a cup and offered a biscuit from a plate with a paper doily.

'Well, Detective Inspector, as you've already guessed, Kieran Wells – an assumed name, by the way - was ex-military. He was a double agent and you'll not come across anyone braver. He had to be pulled when the IRA's Security Council grew suspicious and ordered him to a house in Newry for interrogation. He thought he could bluff his way through it but we knew better. The nutting squad had already lined the garage floor with a plastic sheet and there was only ever going to be one outcome. He'd met the criteria for their Green Book's death sentence. His handlers got him out and back over to the mainland.

As you will have been informed by Dr Fahy, his appearance had to be altered and a new identity created. He elected to live in Burton-on-Trent because he said no-one would know him there. We found him a safe house until the heat had died down and then moved him to the Fairview Mansions flat – which is where he had been living for years. What we don't know is, was his death related to his military past or was it a common-or-garden murder? We need you to find out for us.'

'But you're MI5. Surely you have the resources to do that yourselves.'

'Well, first of all you must remember that we are a wing of the Counter Terrorist structure – the Force Research Unit - that does not officially exist. Secondly, our role is to act on information we receive; we don't actually do the gathering. Thirdly, and most importantly, the investigation into Kieran Wells's death must appear to be conducted by a civilian organisation – the police. Remember what I've just said about score-settling? If any of the three sides get the idea that the military are on the case with an intent to exact revenge, then it's no holds barred. And with your military background in covert ops, George, who better?'

Batt finished his coffee and placed the cup back on the tray.

'Where do I even begin to unravel all of this?'

'I can give you a helping hand with where to start. A certain prominent Catholic – let's for the sake of argument call him "Martin" – has volunteered the name of the IRA's Ops Commander who was sent over here when they changed tack in the eighties and started attacking mainland targets. Apparently, if anyone knows who might have a score to settle, he will.'

'And will he talk? Has Martin given him the OK?'

'Ah, it's not quite that simple. This man is in a care home. He has the beginnings of dementia. Catch him on a good day and you might get something out of him. How do you fancy a spell in a care home, George? Might be good preparation for when your own time comes.'

He got up and pulled a large envelope from out of a filing cabinet.

'Some homework, I'm afraid,' said O'Brien. 'Rules and regulations for care homes. I know you're a well qualified medic from your army days but you won't, for example, be allowed to dish out medicines. We need to stay on the right side of the law.'

Batt raised his eyebrows and O'Brien smiled.

'We've given you a new identity. You're now George James. There are some background notes in here,' he said, handing the package to Batt. 'Speaking of keeping on the right side of the law, we can't have the tax payers paying your police salary as well as the bit you earn as a carer, so when the care home pay the agency I've arranged for it to be forwarded to a charity. With your agreement I thought the Lymphoma Association would be appropriate?'

Batt felt a familiar pain in his chest.

O'Brien studied him for a while before saying, 'She seems to have been a special person, George.'

'She was as special person,' replied Batt. 'A very special person.'

'Come on, let's go and find something to eat. We can continue our discussion later.'

'Just one small thing,' said Batt getting up off his seat. He could certainly do with a meal. Breakfast seemed a long time ago.

'Shoot,' said Smith.

'How am I expected to work under cover in a care home when my boss knows nothing about it? I mean, her red stillettos will be twitching.'

Smith looked at him and smiled.

'Oh I'm sure we can come up with something. I recommend the chicken and broccoli bake. Your favourite, I believe.'

This time Batt did not look surprised.

'One more thing,' he said. 'When DI Mills reads the autopsy report he'll reach the same conclusion as me about Kieran Wells. What happens if our paths cross?'

O'Brien had already picked up his sun glasses and was shepherding Batt out into the corridor.

'Hayfever,' he explained. 'They're always mowing the damn grass. In answer to your first point, we'll find a way – leave it to us. And as for DI Mills let's just say he may not be given quite the same autopsy report as the one you've been reading.'

With that he led Batt through the entrance hall and out into the summer heat.

They walked across a grassed quadrangle between three-storey accommodation blocks. Many of the windows were wide open, a few with clothes drying on the cills. Someone was listening to dance music, the sort that had a repetitive bass sound. Baz had once tried to explain the different styles to him: 4-beat, Big Beat, Breakbeat Hardcore, Nu School Breaks.... He couldn't remember the rest. As far as he was concerned it was all the same thump, thump, thump.

He realised O'Brien had been asking him something.

'Sorry. I was miles away. I didn't realise torture was still allowed.'

'Torture?' O'Brien looked uneasy.

'Some poor devil is being forced to listen to that row coming from over there.' He nodded towards where the music was coming from.

"Oh that? You learn to tune out after a while. The kids are always playing it. I believe the Americans did use music as a form of torture during their War on Terror. Britney Spears, David Gray and Eminem... I imagine it must have been pretty effective.

Anyway, I was asking you about life in the police force. You must miss the adrenaline rush of Afghanistan.'

'Not that you'd notice. You can only live on the edge for so long. When you wake up in the morning and find your hands are shaking, that's the time to get out.'

They had reached the Officers' Mess. O'Brien held the door for him and Batt entered a world of silver service, port and elitism.

He couldn't wait to get back to Burton.

Chapter 5

A couple of days later Batt was at his desk when the internal phone rang. He shifted a pile of folders to get to it, relieved by the interruption. He and his team had been making some progress and had marked a few cases as worthy of following up.

'Batt,' he announced.

'DI Batts. You're to come to my office now,' said the Chief Constable.

She did not sound friendly.

Batt took a final swig of cold coffee, picked up his jacket from the back of his chair, and set off.

Ignoring the red light he opened the door and walked in. The first thing he saw was the look of quiet satisfaction on Ms. P. Foster-Goode's face. The second thing, sitting in a corner, was his Federation rep with an empty coffee cup in his hand.

'Detective Inspector, I have had a serious complaint made about you by a member of the public. There has been an allegation you have used excessive force and threats to obtain a false confession from someone who was subsequently jailed for six months.'

Batt was lost for words and looked to his rep for some sort of protest. Instead, all he got was a shrug of the shoulders.

'Who made the complaint?' he asked when he saw he was not going to get any support.

'I am not at liberty to disclose that, as you well know. Under the Police Conduct Regulations 2010 I am officially suspending you from duty until further notice pending an internal investigation. Moving forwards you will receive confirmation in writing within thirty days. You are to hand over all police equipment, collect any personal possessions from your office and you will then be escorted to your car. Go and spend some gardening leave with your clocks.'

Batt was halfway across the car park when his phone rang. He dumped his carrier bag into the arms of the escorting officer and fished it out of his pocket. It was a withheld number. He was in two minds about answering it but pressed the green button anyway. It was a familiar voice.

'Batt. Meet me in half an hour at the little tea shop in your village. We have things to discuss.'

And with that O'Brien disconnected before Batt had had time to ask whether the call was just lucky timing or insider knowledge.

'Come on Clayton, haven't got all day. You can put that lot in the boot for me. And can you tell Blue team I've gone for a walk and may be some time?'

He had parked in the bay behind his cottage and walked across the road to the village tea rooms. The building faced the village green with its medieval butter cross, or 'gazebo' as Batt was in the habit of calling it. Rumour had it that Dr Johnson and his father had sold books from under its arches. Customers at the neighbouring pub were sitting outside having a liquid lunch and enjoying the weather. One or two regulars waved to Batt as he approached.

His entrance was greeted by the tinkling of a bell and the smell of freshly baked quiche. He scanned the room until he saw O'Brien over in the corner. The place was quiet, the early morning get-together of mothers who'd dropped their children off at the village school having ended, and the lunch-time invasion of the isolated who worked from home yet to begin.

O'Brien stood up and shook hands.

'Sorry about the gardening leave, George. It was the best way we could think of to acquire your services. And before you say it you don't need to worry about you pension. There will be nothing on your records about the suspension.'

The waitress came over and Batt ordered coffee and a low-fat scone.

'So who did you get to file the complaint?' he asked.

'Remember the name Ben Rogers?'

Batt remembered it only too well. The runt of a litter of seven, Ben Rogers had stolen an elderly lady's bag from outside her home and given her a black eye in the process. Batt had returned the compliment when he'd arrested him.

'Says you assaulted him. Wouldn't be true would it George?'

'He was going to deny it but he was guilty. We found the woman's purse under his bed and a pawn ticket for her husband's wedding ring she kept in it. The blow to his head must have jogged his memory and he told us where to look. He didn't file a complaint – not after he was told Big Ali was a friend of the vic and that he wasn't too happy.'

'Big Ali?'

'Aye. Big Ali is the local Mr Big. We have a mutual agreement: we don't ask too many questions about where the stuff on his market stall comes from and in return he keeps his ear to the ground for us.'

O'Brien took a sip of coffee and Batt turned his attention to his scone, slicing it in half and applying a liberal amount of butter from the tiny earthenware pot. It was some moments before either spoke.

'Right George, let's get down to business. As you now know, Kieran Wells was a double agent for us operating in Northern Ireland in the nineties. He had gained a senior position within the IRA and using the intel he supplied MI5 were able to thwart several atrocities – some that would have been on the same scale as the Omagh bombing. It was only when Michael Haughey, the IRA quartermaster for Newry, put two and two together and worked out that it was Kieran who had been supplying him with damp fertiliser for the bomb-making unit, that we had to pull him out.'

Batt flicked a few crumbs off his trousers.

'Ammonium nitrate fertiliser? I thought they used Semtex.'

'Only when they could get hold of it. We had a few successes intercepting their supply ships. They had less trouble bringing in bags of fertiliser from the South. We knew when a load had been delivered because there was an increased demand in coffee grinders in local shops.'

Seeing the look on Batt's face he explained, 'They used coffee grinders to grind the fertiliser to dust. Once they'd done that it had a shelf life of just a few days – but much less if the stuff was a little damp before they started. That's what got Wells into trouble. The stuff he acquired for them rarely detonated.

I'm feeling peckish. Shall we order lunch? Back in a minute.'

He got up and went over to the counter.

'Are we too early to order lunch?' he asked.

He was told there were fresh quiches just out of the oven. They came with a side salad and rice.

'OK with you, George?'

Batt nodded his agreement and O'Brien returned with cutlery wrapped in a paper napkin. Before he sat down he reached into his pocket and produced a phone.

He handed it to Batt saying, 'Keep this with you at all times. The only number it will ring is mine. The unlock code is 2288 – BATT on the numerical keypad. Nice village. Been here long?'

'Since I left the army. But I expect you know that?'

O'Brien's face gave nothing away.

'The cottage was on the market and had been for some time. It needed quite a bit doing to it. The owners were moving abroad and keen to sell. We got it for a decent price but even so it used up most of my savings. We spent the best part of a year stripping it out, rewiring, re-plastering, new plumbing, new windows and doors, whilst I sat exams to join the Force.'

'So why the police? I thought you lot joined security companies when you left the army.'

'You can credit Pete Jones for that. I was all for trying something completely different – something where I was my own boss and not part of an institution. Pete phoned me one day to say he had joined the police based in nearby Burton and that they were recruiting more officers and how did I fancy it. I told him I didn't but, to be honest, when I thought about it it did have its attractions. It seemed to be playing to my strengths. You know, gathering intel and using it to help maintain law and order. And I'd liked working for Pete in Afghanistan. He wasn't your typical Rupert who relied on his RSM to see him through. Pete was a natural leader who soon gained your respect. He was young but as they say 'if you're good enough, you're old enough'.'

He broke off when their lunch arrived.

O'Brien waited for the waitress to disappear before getting down to business.

'The IRA's Opps Quartermaster on the mainland was a man named Tommy McCole. He had been one of their Newry Security Council members – the so-called nutting squad. According to Kieran Wells, he was a decent man, one who insisted on firm evidence before passing sentence on a tout. Believe it or not, the IRA was not run by a bunch of thugs and any members who fell short of its code of conduct were dealt with.

Anyway, when in the late 1970s the IRA's strategy for terrorism changed from bombing Irish targets to bombing mainland targets, McCole was sent to England to oversee the campaign. He operated from a place near Bakewell in north Derbyshire not far from the home of Maurice Oldfield our ex-head of MI6. McCole was one of our "red lights" but even so we learned very little about his activities.

We were pretty sure he supplied the car bomb that was meant to kill Oldfield at the family home of Meadow Place Farm, and also the huge bomb hung on the wall outside his London home in Marsham Court. Then there was an arson attack on St Matthew's Church in Westminster, where Oldfield was sometimes the organist. Mind you, things were made easier for the IRA because – believe it or not - Oldfield's London address was listed in "Who's Who" and his mother's phone number at the farm was listed in the local directory.'

He sighed and lifted a piece of quiche to his mouth.

'We attributed other bombings to his organising, bombings such as the attack on the Attorney General's home in Wimbledon. He almost certainly had some role in the Harrods car bomb in '83 and the Brighton bombing a year later.

Maurice Oldfield died in 1981 but we think McCole was the one who supplied firearms for the Lichfield railway station attack that killed one off-duty soldier and badly injured two others in June 1990. Oldfield had trained at their Whittington barracks in the 1940s, so maybe not a coincidence. In fact we almost caught the driver and planter but they legged it across the railway lines and escaped through a builder's yard just before an armed response unit could get there.

Then when the 1997 ceasefire came into effect McCole just dropped off the radar. According to our Stormont source he is now in a care home near Uttoxeter.'

After rounding up the last of his meal, he wiped his mouth with the serviette and sat back.

'So there you have it. What do you think?'

'I think the two men parked across the road in the black BMW are scoping us out. Are they yours?'

O'Brien did not make the mistake of looking round but shook his head.

'I assumed they were with you. McCole is in a place called "Mount View Nursing Home". Here's a copy of your CV. You best make yourself familiar with it – you start on Monday. No need for an interview – you're an agency employee.'

He got up and made his way to the counter to pay the bill. The owner laughed at something he said as Batt finished his coffee and joined him at the door.

'Remember to keep that phone with you at all times. When you learn something let me know.'

The bell tinkled as the first of the lunchtime regulars arrived. O'Brien caught the door before it closed and, with a farewell wave, made his way down the steps and round the corner.

The BMW edged slowly away from the kerb and also disappeared from sight, leaving Batt to make his way home to contemplate the dubious pleasure of working with those with confused souls.

It was later that evening and beginning to get dark when he was returning from his customary jog around the village that he saw the car parked down a side street. He slowed to a walk and bent as if to tie up a shoelace, studying the vehicle. It didn't appear that anyone was in it so he continued. Even with the windows closed there was the unmistakable smell of weed coming from it. Whoever it was that had been watching him earlier clearly wasn't a professional. He continued down to the church and took a short cut through the churchyard and across a field before approaching his cottage from the rear. His car was there in the parking space but beyond it he noticed his gate was slightly open. He edged forwards, keeping firstly to the line of sycamore trees and then to the wall that separated his property from his neighbour's. Her 4x4 wasn't there so presumably she was working nights at the A&E where she was a nurse. Batt crept along on her side of the wall until he was level with the end of his workshop. There was a strong smell of weed.

He crouched there and listened for a while until he heard someone cough and a whispered instruction to keep quiet. Two of them, then. He crept back to the shared driveway and without trying to conceal his presence walked through his gate and down the steps. Predictably a figure dressed all in black moved out from behind the summerhouse and blocked his path. Batt continued to approach him, smiling.

'You're in the wrong place,' he said. 'The children's play area is up the road.'

The man swung a haymaker at Batt. He was expecting it and ducked under it, bringing his head up under the man's chin. There was a satisfying crunch followed by a spout of blood as the man bit through his own tongue. He was in mid scream when Batt kicked him hard in the groin. The man's eyes rolled in his head as he sank to the floor, where he stayed curled up and moaning. Batt stepped over him and rounded the corner to come face to face with the second attacker. This one was holding a knife – but holding it all wrong.

'No mate,' admonished Batt, 'you need to hold the knife like an extension to your hand. If you hold it like you are then you've got to take a swing at me and I'll see it coming in time to react. Look, I'll show you.'

The second man duly obliged with a wild swing. Batt rocked back on his heels out of range and, with his assailant off balance, gave him a good shove towards the nearest tree. The knife clattered to the ground as man and tree made contact. Batt moved quickly to pick it up off the path before delivering a hefty blow to the kidneys. He joined his mate on the floor. Batt stood over him with one foot on the man's head, grinding his heel into the scalp.

'Who sent you?'

When there was no reply Batt said, 'I'll start by breaking your little finger, then I'll break another and another until you tell me.'

When there was still no answer Batt knelt down and bent the finger backwards until he heard a crack. The man howled in pain which was rewarded with more grinding of shoe on scalp.

'I'll ask you again,' said Batt. 'Who sent you?'

'No-one sent us,' said the first man, propping himself up against the summerhouse wall. 'We were told you'd framed Ben Rogers.'

Batt ignored the retching coming from the one whose finger he'd broken and turned to his accomplice.

'Ben Rogers was not framed. Her handbag was found in his flat. A few months in His Majesty's was less than he deserved – not for nicking a few quid but for what he did to his victim. The old lady he attacked has suffered ever since and will probably end her life in fear of it happening again. She's ended up with a life sentence. Ben Rogers, on the other hand, got free bed and board for six months and is now a free man. Your mother still alive?'

The man nodded.

'Next time it might be her. Be careful about taking the law into your own hands or you might get hurt. By the way, is it Rogers who's your supplier?'

He was met with a questioning look.

'The weed. Is it Rogers who's now supplying your neck of the woods?'

He was given another nod.

'You and your little friend better make your way home before I give you a taste of what Rogers has coming to him. Oh, and I hope your car's paperwork is up-to-date because I'll be checking it out on the PNC.'

Batt continued up his path to his back door, stooping to pat the neighbour's cat on his way and making a mental note to deadhead Fran's roses. They looked in need of a little tlc.

His visitors moved painfully off, holding various parts of their anatomy. His sixth sense told him there had been a third person waiting for him but if there had he had presumably thought twice about getting involved. Batt stood in his doorway watching his attackers disappear down the lane, and smiled to himself.

'Not exactly in the same league as the Taliban,' he reflected.

He went inside and deposited the knife in his kitchen drawer before locking up and going upstairs for a shower.

When he came down again a few minutes later he made his way to the kitchen and got some supper. "Melon Surprise" Fran had named it, the surprise being that he'd had it every night since they had moved to the village and finally settled down to a normal existence.

Being a soldier's wife was tough. You were on your own for long periods, sometimes not knowing where your partner was or when you would next see him. Fran had coped better than most. She lived two lives, one when he was away on a tour and one when he was home. She had had some good friends who had accepted there would be times when she wouldn't be with them until he had returned to wherever he had been posted next – often Afghanistan.

Looking back, Batt could see it took a lot of courage to cope with the life she had chosen to lead. To live with the fear that an RSM could come knocking on the door at any moment with bad news was something that only now he was able to appreciate. The irony was it had not been the

RSM who had come with bad news about him but their GP who had delivered the devastating news about her.

He got up and closed the curtains before sitting down to read for a few minutes. His thoughts, though, kept returning to the meeting with O'Brien.

This Tommy McCole had been a leading figure in the IRA but he was now being allowed to live out his days in a residential home in Staffordshire. The intelligence agencies had been made aware of his presence by the IRA but had not made any move against him. If anything they seemed to be protecting his whereabouts. Perhaps O'Brien was right, that those who had been involved in the Troubles might want to settle old scores before they died and in so doing would trigger a renewed period of sectarian violence at a time when the political map in the province was changing. Tommy McCole seemed to be a man who held information others would dearly love to get their hands on.

He gave up trying to read, said goodnight to Fran's photograph and went upstairs to bed.

Chapter 6

By the time Batt had familiarised himself with forty-eight care home policies he was more than ready for some clock therapy. He had spent the best part of two whole days bent over the desk in his study learning about policies such as Safeguarding, Medication Management, Restraint, and Falls Reporting, and some less obvious ones such as Assistive Technology, Weather Policy and Pet Therapy. He wondered why anyone would want to learn all this just to be paid the Living Wage. For many of the care assistants, English would not even be their first language. And all this before they even set foot in a place and came face-to-face with all the problems associated with looking after the elderly, many of whom had the complexities of dementia.

He put O'Brien's notes back in the envelope, stretched, and made his way downstairs.

Out in the garden all was peaceful. Insects were doing their rounds and in the distance the church bell ringers were practising.

Batt sat on the bench, taking in the last rays of the sun, sipping at a glass of elderberry cordial whilst skimming through clock auction sites on his laptop. No that he needed any more clocks just at that moment but if a good one came up then it would be silly to let it go without bidding. There was one, for example, that he'd noticed coming up at a Nottingham auction. It was a brass-faced eight-day by a good London maker. It had a moon phase, strike-silent dial, date wheel and it struck on the half-hours as well as the hours. The mahogany case was in excellent condition, with lots of inlay and stringing. He made a mental note of the auction date and worked out roughly what time the lot number would be coming up.

Auctioneers got through about one hundred lots per hour, although this particular Nottingham auctioneer tended to be slower than most. Where some auctioneers relied upon speed and excitement to create lively bidding , this one was languid and calm and spoke in a very measured way.

He then checked his emails, automatically deleting the usual crop from retail outlets, before reading those from his colleagues at Burton. He was pleased to see his team in particular were being very supportive; he also felt guilty about the deceit.

He took another sip from his glass and thought about O'Brien and what he'd said about the possible circumstances surrounding Kieran Wells's murder at Fairview Mansions. The use of a truth drug put it into a different league to most murders. The fact Wells had been a double agent for the Brits during the Troubles was the most obvious line to follow. O'Brien had said neither the IRA, nor the British Army, nor the RUC wanted to see any final mopping up operations now that Stormont was at last providing a political solution to the violence. Well maybe he was right about them as organisations but that did not mean an individual within them hadn't gone rogue.

And this man "Martin" who had put O'Brien on to Tommy McCole in the care home – how trustworthy was he? Was it actually he who wanted to settle old scores? In which case who else had Martin told about Tommy's knowledge of who had done what? The Real IRA, for example, had always been opposed to the Good Friday Agreement and had wanted to continue the fight. Had Martin also put them on to Tommy in the hope they could supply him with more names? It seemed to Batt that not only was he going to have to somehow see if McCole could help him by pointing the finger at Kieran Wells's murderer but that he also had to make sure no-one else was trying to tap McCole.

He decided an early night was on the cards. It would be his first day in the morning. A 6:00am start. He went back into the kitchen, rinsed his glass, and locked up, and after blowing Fran a kiss, made his way upstairs.

****

It was going to be another very warm day. The overnight temperature had hardly dipped and Batt could feel the stickiness in the air that suggested thunder storms were not far away. The Mount View care home was only a fifteen minute drive from where he lived, and set in its own pleasant grounds in the countryside. From here it was possible to look down the valley towards the race course and the market town of Uttoxeter. Sadly Uttoxeter was not the bustling town it had once been when the weekly cattle market had taken place. New agricultural regulations had made it unviable and the market had closed, to be replaced by a supermarket and some token low-cost houses. The result was that farmers now had to trail all the way up to Leek to buy and sell livestock. Not only was it longer for the animals to be stuck in the back of a cattle wagon, but it took a huge chunk out of a farmer's working day.

Batt drew up into the car park and turned the engine off. He sat for a moment looking round. The house itself had at one time been quite grand. It looked Victorian, but now with several modern single storey additions. Most of the curtains, he noticed, were still drawn. There were well tended lawns surrounding the building, with several mature trees providing shade to outdoor seating. A squirrel was busy taking nuts from a bird feeder, flicking its tail angrily when a bird tried to join it.

He checked he had O'Brien's phone as well as his own in his pocket, got out and took a deep breath. The next few days and possibly weeks were going to be interesting to say the least.

He approached the main door and rang the bell. It was opened by one of the care home assistants. She was dressed casually in jeans and T-shirt. According to her identity tag her name was Maria. Batt introduced himself and was taken down a corridor to the manager's office. Everything seemed quiet except for muffled sounds coming from what Batt assumed to be the kitchen further down getting ready for breakfast.

The manager looked up as he was shown in.

"Office" was to stretch the imagination. Batt would have called it a cupboard under the stairs. She took off her glasses and smiled, introducing herself as Kate.

'You must be George James. Thank you for joining us, George. The agency speaks very highly of you. We're so short staffed at the moment and now one of our team has recently had an operation on her back so she will be out of action for a while. You'll find everyone is very friendly, if a little rushed off their feet.'

She handed Batt his name tag and looked over his shoulder to address Maria who was still hovering.

'Maria, can I ask you to show George around and to have him shadow you for the morning until he finds his feet?'

Maria looked confused.

'Find his feet?' she asked in an accent Batt thought to be Eastern European.

'Until he knows how we do things, Maria.'

'Oh, yes. My English, George, is not good at such expressions.'

'Your English, Maria, is far better than my knowledge of…?'

He raised a eyebrow.

'Romanian. I come here three years ago from Ploiesti. My husband and son they are still in Romania. Come.'

Batt was led down a corridor and into the newer part of the house. There were doors to either side, each one

69

displaying a photograph and occupant's name. At the end of the corridor was a laundry.

'How many residents are there Maria?'

'We have thirty two, many women. Only three men.'

She pointed to the laundry room.

'Here is the washing done. Always lots of it.'

Several machines were already whirring.

She turned and retraced her steps, Batt following on behind looking closely at the names on the doors until he found Tommy McCole's. His photograph showed a thin face that bore a distant, faraway look. Maria's next comment explained why.

'All on here have dementia. Upstairs we have people who are OK but can't move good.'

They had arrived back to the original part of the building with its ornate plaster-work and high ceilings. A rather grand staircase was to the left along with a lift, whilst on the right was the day room where most of the residents seem to have been herded. It was as Batt had imagined – orange plastic armchairs arranged around three of the walls, with a small tv at the far end, its sound muted. The majority of those in there appeared to be asleep, one or two were reading and, over the far side, a couple were chatting. Batt scanned the room until he found a face that matched the photograph. Tommy McCole was watching him intently whilst holding up a mobile phone. Maria followed Batt's gaze.

'That is Tommy. He always look at new people. Sometimes he has phone and he take a picture. He is a nice man but he teach me to swear. He get me in trouble. On first day I greet visitors with 'Hello Gitface' It was what Tommy tell me you say. Then he tell me Mrs Asted is said 'Arsehead'. I nearly get sack.'

She laughed.

'Soon it is breakfast but first I show you upstairs rooms.'

Batt followed her out and up the stairs.

'What is Ploiesti like, Maria?'

'Oh it has a lot of oil for many years. Many people worked for oil companies but now many leave to live away because not so much oil made. Many come to England where money is OK. My husband he still works for oil but he not paid much.'

'Do you miss it?'

'I miss it, yes.'

She pointed out the various rooms as they walked before stopping suddenly. Batt looked out of the stone mullioned window to the view with Uttoxeter below them in the distance.

'Sometimes I wish I could be at home with family. Sometimes I am not treated well here.'

She came over to join him.

'Ploiesti is big town now. It used to be size of Uttoxeter but oil made it grow. It was very important town in First War so the British destroyed it. Then also in Second War because Germans need our oil.'

She turned to look at him.

'One day you come and meet my family and we show you Ploiesti. It is nice place.'

There were tears in her eyes.

'I'd like to,' said Batt.

'We go now and help with breakfast. Some eat in dining room but many eat in lounge. You can help me serve in lounge.'

As they reached the bottom of the stairs Kate called to him from her office.

'When breakfast is over, George, could you pop in and I'll just go through a few things with you. And by the way, watch out for Hilda. She's the tall lady – usually sits by the window. If she's not liking the look of your face she'll swing her stick at you. Not good if you've got a bowl of cereal and a cup of tea in your hands at the time.'

'Will do,' said Batt and he went off in search of Maria in the lounge.

Breakfast soon arrived, wheeled in on a large trolley by one of the staff. Batt poured cereal into bowls, added milk and grabbed some spoons. The staff took it round to the residents, putting plastic bibs on most of them. Some had to be helped to feed. One clearly was not in the mood for cornflakes, tipping her bowl onto the floor before folding her arms defiantly. The mess was cleaned up and things continued without further interruption.

Batt looked up to see how many more servings were needed and noticed Tommy McCole waving him over.

'I'll take this one to Tommy,' he said, and went over to him.

'Morning Tommy. Breakfast for you.'

What McCole said surprised him.

'Ex military?'

'Yes. How did you know?

Batt put the bowl down on the tray and handed over a spoon.

He was met with a grin before McCole said, 'I could tell by the way you walked. Straight back. Knew as soon as I saw you.'

He waved the spoon in front of Batt's nose.

"I hope you make tea up to army strength. The stuff these lassies dish out is like maid's water.'

Batt grinned.

'I'll see if I can educate them for you Tommy. Will you be wanting toast after your cereal?'

'Aye. And I like it the same colour as my tea.'

'Course I will, Tommy. By the way I hear you nearly got Maria the sack on her first day.'

'Just a wee bit of fun. No harm in it. They'd never sack her, she's too good. Anyway they'd have a job to find someone else. Who'd do their job for the money they're paid? That's why so many of them are foreign. The Brits won't do the work. Will you come and talk to me, like, when you've the time? These women have nothing interesting to say. Get on my nerves, so they do."

I'd better go back and help with breakfast. Where will you be?'

Batt stood up.

'Where will I be? Given the choice son I'd be half way down the A50, but chances are I'll be exactly where I am now. Unless they've dragged me off to sit on the toilet until I produce some results.'

Batt got back to the breakfast trolley.

'Maria. Isn't Tommy supposed to have dementia?'

She looked up.

'It seem to come and go. You know? Sometime he very confused but sometime he seem OK. You take this to Hilda there. But mind sticks. She not in good mood today.'

Later that morning Batt found himself back in the lounge. Apparently the entertainments co-ordinator had organised a game of catch the balloon. All was going well until there was a squabble about who was meant to catch it. One of the combatants suddenly pulled a knitting needle from her bag and burst it. A smattering of applause broke out around the room. Batt couldn't help but smile. Rebels without a cause. Undeterred, the organiser inflated another one and threw it in the direction of Hilda. With a swipe of her stick she batted it away, following it with language that wouldn't have been out of place on a building site.

There was a gasp from a curled-up ancient sitting next to her who then shouted, 'Hilda Meadows. You do not use language like that in my classroom. Go to the headmistress this instant.'

Hilda eyeballed her for a second and was about to do to her what she'd just done to the balloon when Batt arrived to intervene.

'Now Hilda. Let's have none of that. We've all got to get on together haven't we.'

Hilda lowered her eyes and Batt turned to go. He gave a sigh of relief just as something hard made contact with his ankle bone.

Batt let out a howl and heard, 'I will not have people yelling like that in my classroom. You too will go and see the headmistress.'

'See you down there,' said Hilda, and even had the cheek to wink at him.

Hilda was going to have to be watched.

The balloon game ended just as tea and biscuits arrived. Batt went over and sat next to Tommy.

'Didn't they teach you self defence in the army?'

'Aye, but how to disarm a Taliban with a knife, not an old lady with a stick. Can I get you tea and a biscuit?'

'Just tea, George. I'm supposed to be diabetic.'

When he returned Tommy asked him about his army days. Batt described life in Afghanistan and jollied it up with details of one or two raids.

'And what about you, Tommy? What did you do before you moved over here?'

'I left school at sixteen and started work for a farming supply business before joining a different kind of organisation.'

He sipped his tea, lost in thought.

'They were dangerous times in the North. I was born in Cookstown – peaceful compared to places like Derry and Omagh. A bit of a backwater, perhaps, and best known for its cement works and sausages. Cookstown sausages were unbeatable. Ever tried them?'

Batt shook his head.

'Anyways, I moved to Belfast looking for work. Plenty of it if, like me, you could operate a JCB, of course. Then in the mid seventies the company policy changed and I was moved to the mainland with a bit of a promotion to sugar the pill.'

'Did you leave family behind?'

'I did, but not what you might call close family. Ma died when I was seven and me Da was one of the thirteen killed in the Bloody Sunday massacre in 1972. I was with him when he died. A bullet in the back. It was a peaceful protest, you know. None of us were armed but the soldiers were out in force and looking to assert their authority. Why would they have their top brass present just for an ordinary protest? Anyway, it was after that that things got worse for us. Brutality like you wouldn't believe, giving us beatings on the streets and smashing down our doors and ransacking our homes. Some of us were shot, you know, but it never made any headlines.'

His hands were shaking as he recalled the events. Batt gently took the cup from him and placed it on the tray at the side of his chair.

'Do you have any close relatives?'

'Och, come on. We're Catholics. Ma had six brothers and sisters and Da was one of five. I've not been in touch with any of them for years though.'

'And you never thought of going back home?'

McCole was about to reply when the entertainments manager returned and a CD started to play war-time songs, drowning out whatever he might have been going to say. Over the far side Hilda began to sing, encouraging those around her to do the same. Soon most of the room was joining in.

'Funny thing do you not think, George? Most of them can't even remember their own names but they know all the words to the old songs.'

Maria came over and collected the cup.

'I'll give you a hand,' said Batt. He patted McCole on the shoulder and set off round the room.

Pushing the trolley of dirty cups beakers and plates back along the corridor towards the kitchen, Maria said, ' Watch man who sit next to Tommy. Wilf is escape artist. He thinks he is prisoner here. You have good talk with Tommy. He not have many men here to talk to.'

'He was talking about the old days, Maria. Like you I think he misses the place where he was born.' Then he had a thought.

'Are we allowed to take them out? On my day off, could I take Tommy out do you think?'

'I think it OK. Others are taken out by family and friends. You will have to speak to Manager. Tommy does not have anyone come to take him out, although a relative came to see him last week. He not have visitor before.'

'Did he say who he was?'

'He say cousin from Ireland. He was very concerned about Tommy. He ask to see Tommy's room and I take him. Unfortunately Tommy not here. He go to see doctor in hospital. I think doctor is worried about him.'

'Did Tommy know this cousin when he was told about his visit?'

'No. Tommy not having best of days. His cousin tell me he is in England for a meeting and staying in town. He say he will come again soon when Tommy not so forgetful.'

'Would you remember him if he came again?'

Maria manoeuvred the trolley into the kitchen.

'It's Tommy have memory problem, not me,' she said, smiling.

The rest of the day was spent helping with meals and talking through memory books with a couple of the residents. Dementia may have robbed them of the immediate past but not of the distant. One of the two had led a particularly interesting life, having been a member of the British Expeditionary Arctic Team that first raised awareness of global warming. She had gone on to work for Greenpeace, narrowly avoiding death when the ship she was on was sunk in Australian waters. A few visitors had drifted in and out, and one or two of the women had been wheeled off to have their hair and nails done.

Whilst waiting to collect one of them he'd taken the opportunity to have a quick look through the visitors' signing-in book. He couldn't see anyone who'd come to see Tommy, but that didn't mean much. It was easy enough to visit without signing the book if you didn't want your presence recorded.

Just before his shift finished Kate had a quick word to say she hadn't used Batt's agency before but that she was impressed by his knowledge and attitude and that she would like to use them again in the future.

'You'll be lucky,' he thought. He'd thanked her and asked about taking Tommy out.

'I thought he might enjoy a day's fishing,' said Batt. 'He tells me he used to do quite a bit of it when he was younger.'

'I think that would be a lovely gesture,' was the reply. 'He doesn't get out unless he's in the minibus full of women. It will do him good to have a bit of male company. Ask cook for a couple of packed lunches when you know when you're going.'

He had just got to his car when his phone started to ring.

'Good timing,' said Batt. 'I've just finished for the day.'

'And how was your first day?'

'Not bad,' he said, pressing the car's key fob. When he opened the door the heat from inside made him take a step back. He must remember to park in the shade next time.

'Our PoI seemed friendly enough, and surprisingly with it for saying he is supposed to have dementia. I think if I can gain his trust he might be open to giving us some help about the Wells murder.'

'Sounds promising. How do you explain his mental state?'

'Could be early onset dementia I suppose, except according to one of the staff he's either very alert or totally out of it. Not just a touch forgetful. By the way, who's paying his bills?'

'That's what we want you to find out. See if you can get a look at the accounts book. The manager must send bills out to whoever's paying the residents' fees.'

The call was ended and Batt put the phone back into his pocket before getting behind the wheel.

He detoured into Uttoxeter to get some shopping and arrived home with enough time for a barbecue in the garden. His phone rang just as he was about to take a mouthful of chicken and salad. His instinct was to ignore it but he picked it up and looked at the caller display. It was Siobhan.

'Hi George. Hope you've not been wasting your day with those old clocks. I heard on the grapevine that she with the red shoes had put you on gardening leave. I hope you've not been a naughty boy.'

'As if,' he replied.

'Chris Talbot says he's been trying to get hold of you but your phone's been switched off.'

'I think there's a fault with it. The screen keeps lighting up and it seems to be draining the battery. I'll have to take it back to "PhoneConnect" when I've got a minute. You were lucky to get me – I was just about to put it on charge. Anyway, what does Chris want?'

'To tell you DI Mills has arrested a suspect for the murder of Kieran Wells.'

'Oh, and did he give you a name?'

'Ben Rogers'

'Ben Rogers?'

Batt dropped the piece of chicken he was turning over back onto the barbecue.

'Are you joking? Ben Rogers may be a fully paid up member of the Society of Low Life but he isn't a killer!'

'Apparently he was seen skulking around the flats at the time of the murder, and ran off when someone appeared.'

'Skulking around selling drugs, not skulking around waiting to murder someone. Well, good luck to Millsie with making that one stick.'

'Are you going to eat all that chicken yourself?'

'Just how did you know…'

He looked up and saw Siobhan waving to him from the gate.

'Very funny,' said Batt. 'You can join me only if you've bought a bottle of something nice with you. And it better not have any alcohol in it.'

She produced a bottle of elderflower from behind her back and made her way down the path.

'Before we start the pleasantries I want to give you some information that might interest you.'

'Hang on,' said Batt. 'Just let me get you a plate from the kitchen.'

When he returned, Siobhan said, 'The hole in the head was probably made by a Webley .38. Remember the scan we did on Kieran Wells? How it showed up some metal fragments in his abdomen? I had forensics take a look. Guess what? They came from a mortar used by the British army in the 1970s. According to forensics the army experimented with a new alloy which it gave to troops deployed in Northern Ireland to test.'

Batt took a moment to let it sink in. What O'Brien had told him about Wells being a double agent made sense, but why had the intelligence forces allowed him to be in the firing line? Surely he was too valuable an asset to risk killing? He knew from his time in Afghanistan that the use of experimental weapons would be closely monitored and that the intelligence forces would have been informed before they were deployed in order for them to do a post op analysis of the results.

'Well, well,' he finally managed. 'Thanks Siobhan. You do know I'm not assigned to the Wells murder any more?'

'Yes, but when did an inconvenience like that ever get in your way?'

She filled a couple of glasses. 'Cheers, George. By the way, your roses have green fly.'

Chapter 7

Batt had two days off work before starting on night shifts.

He thought it was time he caught up with his team to see what had been happening back at the Station and so put a call through to Baz James.

'Hello, Sir. How are things with you?'

'Fine, Baz. Just spending my time pottering about until Ms. Foster-Goode requests my company. Are you free to meet for tea and cakes?'

'Not today I'm afraid Sir. I'm working lates. But I might know someone who is. Can I ring you back in five minutes?'

He rang off and Batt wandered through to the kitchen to put away the breakfast things. When the phone rang it was Helen.

'You did promise tea and cakes, Sir?'

'Hi Helen. Yes, tea and cakes.'

'Lovely. Where and when, Sir?'

'Are you free this morning?'

'I'm on afternoons today so any time this morning will suit me.'

'How about half ten in Birds on the High Street?'

'Great. It will be nice to see you again, Sir. We're all missing you. See you later.'

He felt oddly moved.

He parked at the Octogan Centre and paid for a couple of hours. His first job was to visit the shop where he'd bought his phone. He walked across the car park and into the indoor shopping centre, buying a copy of "Big Issue" from Alina on the way. She had been selling from her pitch for as long as Batt could remember. Always polite and smiling, even to those who ignored her. They had exchanged a few words about the weather, and he had managed to understand enough from her broken English to learn she was still living in sheltered accommodation on the other side of town.

The centre was fairly quiet. He noticed one or two shop windows advertising Hallowe'en things. When he was a child it would have been fireworks. Hallowe'en had muscled in to fill the gap now that fireworks were considered too dangerous for anyone but official organisers to handle. He wondered if these official organisers had to pass examinations. Level One: sparklers, Level Two: Catherine Wheels, Level Three: Roman Candles. He reached the phone shop before he could work out whether bangers would be a higher Level than rockets, and walked in through the open doors.

The same spiky-haired youth who had sold him the phone was arranging some packets of ear buds on a revolving stand. Several unopened boxes lay scattered around the base. Batt stood and waited until he felt his patience running out.

'Excuse me, Son. Do you know anyone who works here?'

Spiky-Hair finished hanging the last of the box's ear buds before turning to face Batt.

'I do. Is there something you want?'

'Yes. I'd like a phone that actually works properly.'

He held up his mobile and waggled it in front of the puzzled face.

'You sold it to me not long ago. The screen keeps lighting up for no apparent reason and the battery needs recharging every five minutes.'

'Sounds like you've downloaded a virus.'

'I thought it was supposed to be a smart phone.'

'It is.'

'Well it's not that smart then, is it? How did it get a virus?'

'Probably something you've downloaded from the internet, innit.'

He bent down and was about to reach for a fresh box of ear buds when Batt placed his foot on it.

'How do I get rid of the virus?'

'If you leave it with me I'll do it for you. Be about an hour.'

Batt removed his foot from the box and smiled.

'Now there's customer service for you. Your boss would be proud of you.'

Spikey sighed and said, 'I *am* the boss. I own the shop.'

There was not much he could say in reply so waved a farewell and walked out of the Centre and into the main street. The carillon on the market square clock chimed ten. Just time to walk down to B&M before meeting Helen.

He could see Dean's mum busy at one of the tills. He went inside, collected a wire basket, and wandered up and down the aisles collecting a few things that were on his shopping list. He joined the queue and slowly edged forwards. She looked up in between customers and saw him. She broke into a smile and gave a small wave.

When it was his turn he managed to ask how she was doing and how Dean and Kira were. She had, it turned out, been promoted to the check-outs, and Dean was loving working towards his junior coaching badge. And she'd been able to pay for young Kira to go to dance classes on Saturdays in rooms above one of the big stores. Batt told her he was proud of her. She mouthed "thank you" as he bagged his things and left.

On his way back up High Street he called briefly into one or two shops to ask how things were. Shoplifting, he was told, was still on the increase.

Coming out of the last shop he caught a glimpse of a familiar face just before it disappeared suddenly into the nearest doorway. He strolled up and entered, to find Ben Rogers peering out from behind a rack of clothes.

'Ben Rogers. You wouldn't be trying to avoid me by any chance?'

Rogers emerged from his hiding place.

'No Mr Batt. I was just doing some shopping.'

Batt looked around at the displays of ladies underwear.

'So what is it? You into cross dressing now? Must be all that drugs money that's gone to your head.'

'Well Mr Batt I have to admit I didn't think you'd be too pleased to see me. After you was suspended, like. But the thing is, Mr Batt, I can explain everything.'

'Ben.' Batt held up his hands. 'I don't want to hear it. I'm not interested in your complaint to our new Chief Constable'

'You're not? Not even when I tell you I dropped the complaint yesterday?'

'You did?' said Batt. If that was the case then O'Brien must have thought he'd learnt enough, or at least that he would have by the time the Police Complaints panel met to decide whether to drop the charges against him.

'Now let's go and get that tea and cake?'

'Tea and cake, Mr Batt?'

'Yes, Ben. It's what nice people eat sitting down at a table rather than trailing fumes of onions as they gnaw their way through a McPoison whilst walking through the shopping centre. Come on. Follow me. And if you even think about legging it I'll have some officers pay a visit to your flat and leave no stone unturned. Or should that be no negligee unturned.'

They arrived at the confectioners to find Helen waiting outside studying the pastries displayed in the window. She turned as they approached.

Rogers looked nervously up and down the High Street.

'Sorry I'm late. I bumped into Ben here and wanted you to meet him. Ben, this is DC Helen Hastings. Helen, this is Ben Rogers. His name might be familiar to you. Shall we go in?'

'What if I'm seen in here with you Mr Batt?'

'Ben, the sort of people you associate with are hardly likely to come to a place like this. Now in you go.'

The three of them were greeted by a pleasant thirty-something dressed in a smart black skirt and immaculate white blouse. She took them over to a table towards the back of the eating area.

The waitress produced a notepad and pencil.

'Tea and a selection of cakes please,' Batt requested.

'Yes, Sir. Any special dietary requirements?'

Batt looked at the other two who shook their heads.

'I'll be back in a moment.' Then, looking at Rogers she added, 'Would you like me to take your coat, Sir?'

'I'm ok.' mumbled Rogers.

The waitress looked quizically in Batt's direction.

'He feels the cold,' said Batt.

When she had left, he raised the subject of Rogers' arrest.

'Well to be honest Mr Batt, and no offence, but I thought the arresting officer was a pillock.'

'And the arresting officer was?'

'Some bloke called Mills. I hadn't met him before. He and his mates smashed my door in at three in the morning and cuffed me. Then they dragged me off to the station and charged me with murder! I mean, Mr Batt, I might accidentally get involved in a bit of shoplifting or breaking and entering but murder? That's a bit out of my league, don't you agree?'

'So what happened?'

'They held me over night in a cell and next morning told me to ring my solicitor because I was going to be sent down for twenty years for what I'd done. I'd never heard of the geezer they said I'd snuffed. Didn't even know where this Fairtrade Mansion place was where I was supposed to have been.'

'Fairview,' said Batt. 'It's called Fairview, not Fairtrade. Fairtrade's something you wouldn't know the meaning of.'

'Right. Anyways next morning my solicitor arrives and this posh tottie comes into the interview room.'

'Posh tottie?'

'Yeh. Got lots of names.'

'Ms. Foster-Goode?'

'Might have been.'

'And then?'

'Well she switches on the tape and says the usual about who's there and what time it is, and then spends an hour questioning me. I have to keep saying "no comment" because I haven't any comment to make! Then she turns to my solicitor and says I'm going to be held for further questioning. He says something like "On what grounds" and she says they have a witness what saw me there at the time the poor bloke was killed. So my solicitor says "It wasn't him" – meaning me. Tottie says the witness is reliable so unless I can prove I wasn't there I'm going to be charged.'

'So. What happened Ben? Why did they release you?'

'Well, my solicitor said he could prove the witness was wrong and I hadn't been there. He said to me "Mr Rogers, roll up your trouser leg." You see, Mr Batt, I was tagged. It was a condition of my early release. When they left the interview room I could hear Tottie shouting at this DI Mills. I won't repeat exactly what she called him but if you ask me it was a bit sexist.'

Batt winked at Helen.

'Sounds like your case load might be increasing DC Hastings.'

He turned back to Rogers.

'Bit of an oversight from the arresting officer, Ben. But why didn't you tell them about your tag when they arrested you?'

'Next morning was Wednesday. They do a full English for breakfast on a Wednesday.'

He grinned and looked around.

'Posh in 'ere Miss ain't it?' he said to Helen.

'Posh? Well, I'm not sure it's posh, it's...erm.'

Batt turned to Helen.

'Now then DC Hastings. Ben here has a bit of a problem.'

'Do I, Mr Batt?'

'Ben's problem is he doesn't seem to be able to keep on the right side of the law. He's no sooner served his six months in prison than he's being picked up by the police for something else. Isn't that right Ben?'

'Well the thing is, Mr Batt, I can't get no job with my past record. No one will give me a chance. Then word gets out that I need some cash and I'm forced back into crime. If I try to say no I'm threatened with violence. And you know what some of 'em are like round here, Mr Batt.'

'A little birdie tells me you graduated to the drugs scene, is that right?'

Rogers didn't look up.

'You know that means you've crossed the line as far as I'm concerned. You started off in petty crime, next thing I know is you've moved on to beating up old ladies, and now here you are dealing drugs to kids.'

He broke off as the waitress arrived with their tea things. She placed her tray on their table and carefully removed the china cups and saucers, together with a pot of tea and a jug of milk. Last to leave the tray was a silver stand containing a selection of fresh cakes.

'Would you like anything else? I will bring a pot of hot water when you've had time to drink your first cup. Would you like a sugar bowl?'

Batt eyed Rogers and nodded.

'Thank you,' he said. 'It looks delicious.'

She smiled and moved off to take an order from an elderly couple who had just arrived and had managed to find an empty table next to the window.

'And what are these little forks for?' said Rogers, picking one up and checking to see whether it was hallmarked.

'They,' said Batt, 'are for cutting up your cake instead of having to shove it in your mouth in one go – like you've just done.'

'Yeh, well, they're only small ain't they?'

'They're called 'fancies'. And it's not the fancies that are small so much as your mouth that's big. Didn't you learn in prison that you had a big mouth?'

Rogers conceded that, yes, he had.

'And don't even think about adding any spoons to whatever you've already got in those enormous pockets. The waitress may not have counted them but I have. Help yourself to a cake.'

Rogers took one and studied his surroundings: dark wood tables with white linen tablecloths, at which were seated groups of mainly elderly people chatting quietly. The décor was of an age gone by, but not in the twee way that some retro tea shops tried to emulate. Birds had simply maintained the ambience that it had always had.

'Shall I be Mum?' asked Helen, reaching over and arranging the cups and plates.

'Ben,' Batt resumed, 'I particularly wanted you to meet DC Hastings because she is what we call a Community Liaison Officer. She has some useful contacts with local employers. She might be able to save your soul. But nothing comes for free. Just as she's got contact with the world of work, you've got contact with the world of crime.'

Rogers studied Helen for a moment.

'I don't think it's that easy. You see, the people I do jobs for won't be happy.'

'Oh I'm sure we can persuade your employer that you're becoming a bit of a liability. Want to give it a try?'

Rogers eyed the cake stand.

'Help yourself,' said Batt.

This time he picked up his fork and grinned.

'There you are, DC Hastings, our Ben is a quick learner.'

Rogers held fork and cake suspended in mid air whilst he thought things over.

'Yeh, I'll give it a try. But only if you promise I won't get turned over by the enforcers.'

'Believe me, Ben, when they realise the police are on to you, your supplier will be glad to get shot.'

Rogers finished his cake, drained his cup, and stood up to leave.

'Thanks Mr Bott. Thanks Miss. I'll have to go. I've got to sign in at the Station at midday.'

They watched him reach the doorway and peer out before hurrying off in the direction of Barr Gates and the police station.

Batt shook his head and turned to Helen.

'Another cup? And don't let those cakes go stale.'

'As if,' she said.

He reached over and poured whilst she chose.

'Shouldn't we be arresting him if he's a serial shoplifter?' she asked, eying the chocolate eclair that was midway between plate and mouth.

'Had we but world enough and time,' was the reply.

'Sir?'

'Andrew Marvell poem. Mind you he was more concerned with having his wicked way with a woman than with some knocked off stuff from Poundland. You're probably right but we have to prioritise, Helen. I dare say a few cheap arrests would help massage Ms. Foster-Goode's crime statistics but it's things like knife crime, child grooming and the drugs scene that do more harm in the community than Rogers helping himself to some freebies.

Rogers may be a bottom feeder and that's where the likes of Big Ali's acquaintances want him to stay, but he could be useful to you. Get to know who the other low lives are and turn them around before the big boys can move them into the drugs game and they won't have their next generation of gofers. It's a bit like a cancer. Cut off the blood supply and it will die.

Anyway, he's all yours. He could be a useful pair of eyes and ears. Intel. It's something you need if you want to start climbing the greasy promotion pole. Don't expect him to give up the petty crime, though. Just turn a blind eye to it because whilst he's in the criminal loop he can pick up information. Who knows, make a name for yourself in the Force and you could turn out to be another Foster-Goode. Mind you you'd have to learn how to walk in red stilettos.'

The waitress appeared and asked if they'd like their tea hotting up. Helen looked her watch and said she wasn't in a rush if Batt wasn't.

'So how's things with the team?'

'Oh, OK I guess. Baz has a new girlfriend. He has her photo pinned up on the door of his locker. Keeps sneaking a look when he thinks no-one is watching. Chris is settling in. I think he's gradually getting used to our sense of humour. He did a good job following up on some of the ism cases. I think Pete James feels the reports are good enough to send to the CPS.

Look, Sir, I don't want to pry but wasn't it Rogers who got you suspended?'

'Yes,' replied Batt.

'Don't you think it was a bit risky talking to him? You could be accused of interfering with a witness if anyone has seen you.'

'Well for a start Helen you can confirm I did nothing of the sort, and secondly Ben Rogers withdrew his complaint yesterday.'

He saw her concerned expression.

'No, it was nothing to do with me. God works in a mysterious way. I'm sure we'll have an explanation in due course.'

She looked relieved.

'Does that mean you'll be back at work soon, Sir? It really isn't the same without you.'

'Hopefully Ms Foster-Goode will be throwing a welcome back party for me before too long. So how's DI Mills getting on with the Kieran Wells case?'

'Not much progress from what I can tell. Rumour has it the Chief is getting a bit impatient with him and his team.'

She checked her watch and said she'd better be on her way.

'Thanks for the tea, Sir, and for passing Rogers over to me. I appreciate it. See you soon.'

'Yes, see you soon. Pass my regards on to the team.'

'Will do, Sir.'

Once she'd left, Batt paid the bill and made his way back to the phone shop. His two hours parking would be up soon and he knew from experience that if the CCTV recorded him leaving past his time he'd get a fine through the post.

Spikey, he was told, had gone for his lunch and instead a girl in full Goth regalia dealt with him.

'I left my phone with him about an hour ago. Did the manager say what the problem was?'

'Virus.'

'Not someone tapping the phone?'

She looked at him as though she couldn't believe anyone would want to waste their time tapping his phone.

'No. No tell-tale little green dot at the top of the screen and it shut down OK. Just a common virus. Happens a lot. You might think about getting yourself a VPN though. Anyway he's cleaned it up for you. No charge, he said.'

Batt was impressed.

'He seems very young to be owning his own business. Did he learn from his parents or a friend perhaps?'

'Went to uni, I think. Got an MSc, whatever that is.'

She smiled and held the door for him as he left.

'Would you like anything else? I will bring a pot of hot water when you've had time to drink your first cup. Would you like a sugar bowl?'

Batt eyed Rogers and nodded.

'Thank you,' he said. 'It looks delicious.'

She smiled and moved off to take an order from an elderly couple who had just arrived and had managed to find an empty table next to the window.

'And what are these little forks for?' said Rogers, picking one up and checking to see whether it was hallmarked.

'They,' said Batt, 'are for cutting up your cake instead of having to shove it in your mouth in one go – like you've just done.'

'Yeh, well, they're only small ain't they?'

'They're called 'fancies'. And it's not the fancies that are small so much as your mouth that's big. Didn't you learn in prison that you had a big mouth?'

Rogers conceded that, yes, he had.

'And don't even think about adding any spoons to whatever you've already got in those enormous pockets. The waitress may not have counted them but I have. Help yourself to a cake.'

Rogers took one and studied his surroundings: dark wood tables with white linen tablecloths, at which were seated groups of mainly elderly people chatting quietly.

The décor was of an age gone by, but not in the twee way that some retro tea shops tried to emulate. Birds had simply maintained the ambience that it had always had.

'Shall I be Mum?' asked Helen, reaching over and arranging the cups and plates.

'Ben,' Batt resumed, 'I particularly wanted you to meet DC Hastings because she is what we call a Community Liaison Officer. She has some useful contacts with local employers. She might be able to save your soul. But nothing comes for free. Just as she's got contact with the world of work, you've got contact with the world of crime.'

Rogers studied Helen for a moment.

'I don't think it's that easy. You see, the people I do jobs for won't be happy.'

'Oh I'm sure we can persuade your employer that you're becoming a bit of a liability. Want to give it a try?'

Rogers eyed the cake stand.

'Help yourself,' said Batt.

This time he picked up his fork and grinned.

'There you are, DC Hastings, our Ben is a quick learner.'

Rogers held fork and cake suspended in mid air whilst he thought things over.

'Yeh, I'll give it a try. But only if you promise I won't get turned over by the enforcers.'

'Believe me, Ben, when they realise the police are on to you, your supplier will be glad to get shot.'

Rogers finished his cake, drained his cup, and stood up to leave.

'Thanks Mr Bott. Thanks Miss. I'll have to go. I've got to sign in at the Station at midday.'

They watched him reach the doorway and peer out before hurrying off in the direction of Barr Gates and the police station.

Batt shook his head and turned to Helen.

'Another cup? And don't let those cakes go stale.'

'As if,' she said.

He reached over and poured whilst she chose.

'Shouldn't we be arresting him if he's a serial shoplifter?' she asked, eying the chocolate eclair that was midway between plate and mouth.

'Had we but world enough and time,' was the reply.

'Sir?'

'Andrew Marvell poem. Mind you he was more concerned with having his wicked way with a woman than with some knocked off stuff from Poundland.

You're probably right but we have to prioritise, Helen. I dare say a few cheap arrests would help massage Ms. Foster-Goode's crime statistics but it's things like knife crime, child grooming and the drugs scene that do more harm in the community than Rogers helping himself to some freebies.

Rogers may be a bottom feeder and that's where the likes of Big Ali's acquaintances want him to stay, but he could be useful to you. Get to know who the other low lives are and turn them around before the big boys can move them into the drugs game and they won't have their next generation of gofers. It's a bit like a cancer. Cut off the blood supply and it will die.

Anyway, he's all yours. He could be a useful pair of eyes and ears. Intel. It's something you need if you want to start climbing the greasy promotion pole. Don't expect him to give up the petty crime, though. Just turn a blind eye to it because whilst he's in the criminal loop he can pick up information. Who knows, make a name for yourself in the Force and you could turn out to be another Foster-Goode. Mind you you'd have to learn how to walk in red stilettos.'

The waitress appeared and asked if they'd like their tea hotting up. Helen looked her watch and said she wasn't in a rush if Batt wasn't.

'So how's things with the team?'

'Oh, OK I guess. Baz has a new girlfriend. He has her photo pinned up on the door of his locker. Keeps sneaking a look when he thinks no-one is watching. Chris is settling in. I think he's gradually getting used to our sense of humour. He did a good job following up on some of the ism cases. I think Pete James feels the reports are good enough to send to the CPS.

Look, Sir, I don't want to pry but wasn't it Rogers who got you suspended?'

'Yes,' replied Batt.

'Don't you think it was a bit risky talking to him? You could be accused of interfering with a witness if anyone has seen you.'

'Well for a start Helen you can confirm I did nothing of the sort, and secondly Ben Rogers withdrew his complaint yesterday.'

He saw her concerned expression.

'No, it was nothing to do with me. God works in a mysterious way. I'm sure we'll have an explanation in due course.'

She looked relieved.

'Does that mean you'll be back at work soon, Sir? It really isn't the same without you.'

'Hopefully Ms Foster-Goode will be throwing a welcome back party for me before too long. So how's DI Mills getting on with the Kieran Wells case?'

'Not much progress from what I can tell. Rumour has it the Chief is getting a bit impatient with him and his team.'

She checked her watch and said she'd better be on her way.

'Thanks for the tea, Sir, and for passing Rogers over to me. I appreciate it. See you soon.'

'Yes, see you soon. Pass my regards on to the team.'

'Will do, Sir.'

Once she'd left, Batt paid the bill and made his way back to the phone shop. His two hours parking would be up soon and he knew from experience that if the CCTV recorded him leaving past his time he'd get a fine through the post.

Spikey, he was told, had gone for his lunch and instead a girl in full Goth regalia dealt with him.

'I left my phone with him about an hour ago. Did the manager say what the problem was?'

'Virus.'

'Not someone tapping the phone?'

She looked at him as though she couldn't believe anyone would want to waste their time tapping his phone.

'No. No tell-tale little green dot at the top of the screen and it shut down OK. Just a common virus. Happens a lot. You might think about getting yourself a VPN though. Anyway he's cleaned it up for you. No charge, he said.'

Batt was impressed.

'He seems very young to be owning his own business. Did he learn from his parents or a friend perhaps?'

'Went to uni, I think. Got an MSc, whatever that is.'

She smiled and held the door for him as he left.

On his way back to the car he made a slight detour to the open market. It occupied most of the market square which had rows of small shops and cafes down either side and the ancient St Modwen's church at the top end. Its carrilon was ringing the half hour.

Batt jinked his way between shoppers and stalls until he found the one he was looking for.

It was piled high with outdoor clothing, the frame of the stall being used to hold up some for display on coathangers.

An overweight man of Asian descent was holding court with some youths in hoodies. They noticed Batt and quickly moved off. The stall holder looked round and half raised a hand in greeting before turning away and rearranging some black puffa jackets.

'DI Batt. Never a pleasure,' he said.

Batt smiled.

'Some nice stock you've got in, Big Ali. All pukka is it? Only I couldn't help but notice that the logo on this Nike fleece is back to front.'

He picked it up and waved it at the man.

'Yeh, well, it's seconds innit.'

'That's alright then. For one terrible moment I thought you'd been ripped off with some counterfeit stock.'

He put the jacket back on the stall and eyed the rest of the merchandise.

'Is there some thing what you came about Mr Batt?'

'Not some*thing* so much as some*one*.'

He took a step closer to Big Ali.

'We have this understanding don't we? You supply me with the odd bit of useful intel and in return I don't ask too many questions about your suppliers. Now what I'm wondering, being as I haven't pursued my line of questioning about the possibility that your genuine branded goods are all fakes, is whether you've got anything to pass on to me about Ben Rogers.'

'Ben who?'

'Because we believe he has graduated from selling a few hookey items down at his local to supplying drugs to those on the Fairview estate. The thing is, Big Ali, we're watching his every move in the expectation that sooner or later he will lead us to his supplier.'

'I don't have nuffin to do with drugs, Mr Batt.'

Batt held up his arms to stop the protest.

'No, I know you don't. But I do know you have a wide circle of friends. It would be a shame if one of them were to be arrested, especially as you've been seen talking to me just now.'

He nodded in the direction of the youths who were leaning up against a cafe window watching them both.

'I'll ask around.'

Batt turned to go and gave him a friendly pat on the shoulder.

He checked his watch and hurried off, nearly colliding with Elsie Goodbody as he rounded the corner by Aitkins Gents Outfitters.

'Mr Batt. Thanks for your help. That young police woman came to have a word and she's going to take me down to the Citizens. Thinks they can help get my loan sorted.'

'Pleased to hear it Elsie. Sorry but I've got to dash. Parking's running out.

Hope Jade and Billy are behaving,' he added over his shoulder.

'Good as gold,' he heard her say.

He made it back to the car with three minutes to spare.

Chapter 8

Batt had actually found himself enjoying his work at Mount View. He had got to know many of the residents and in doing so had developed a genuine respect for them. It was generally a happy place. There were fallings out, of course, as there were in any close community, but on the whole the atmosphere was relaxed and cheerful. These were not people who were simply waiting to die.

He had got used to the routine of daily life there – routine being something those with dementia needed. He kept in regular contact with O'Brien, often phoning on his way home. As yet there wasn't much to report.

He'd managed to take Tommy fishing on the nearby reservoir and had spent a pleasant afternoon with him, the two comfortable in each other's company. He had hired a boat with a small outboard motor and had driven under the causeway to the top end where it was quieter. Batt hadn't pushed Tommy for any information about himself, trying instead to gain his trust by chatting about mundane things. Sometimes one of their lines had bobbed but the fish weren't biting. It didn't matter. The weather was pleasantly warm and both men had enjoyed simply being able to relax.

He was now preparing to take Tommy out again. He'd arranged for the kitchen staff to pack up some food and had brought along some cans of low-alcohol beer for Tommy and elderflower for himself. Tommy was waiting for him when he arrived at the Home, sitting on a bench under one of the trees with Maria. They were both laughing at something going on over by the residents' wing. Batt followed their gaze. Two members of staff were wrestling with Wilf who had one leg out of an open window and was resisting capture by bracing both arms against the wall.

Maria saw him and waved and the pair of them got up and walked over to the car. Maria held out the box containing the lunches.

'It is lovely day again George. I wish I come with you.'

'Thanks Maria,' said Batt, taking the box. 'It's a pity you're working. If you came you might bring us some luck with the fish. We didn't catch a thing last time. Do those two need a hand with Wilf?'

'No. He give up in a minute. He probably try again later.'

She helped Tommy into the car.

'You behave, Tommy McCole. And no swearing at fish.'

Tommy grinned. 'I've got a new one to teach you when I get back.'

He had a finger waggled at him in reply and they set off down the country lanes, not saying much but comfortable in each other's company.

Before long Batt reached Bishop's Bromley and took a right turn up a narrow lane. At the top of the hill was a farm which served coffee and cakes. The cakes were homemade each morning by the farmer and the place had gained a certain reputation with groups of cyclists. Batt pulled into the courtyard and bought himself a slice of coffee cake and a sugar-free scone for McCole. Already the place was busy with groups of lycra-clad enthusiasts dotted about on seats and benches.

'I have nothing against cyclists, Tommy,' said Batt, 'but when you've been stuck behind them for a mile or so you do get fed up with the view of their backsides. Lycra doesn't leave much to the imagination.'

'That reminds me of the old joke. This feller murdered his wife and buried her in the garden. When his mate came round he asked why the man had left her bottom sticking out of the ground. 'Well,' said the man, "I've needed somewhere to park me bike".'

'Billy Connolly?'

'Aye I think you may be right. I'm not into this modern comedy, though, are you? Seems to be all about their personal lives. I went to see Ken Dodd when he was on at Buxton a few years ago. Joke after joke for nearly four hours. People were having to leave before the end in case they missed the last bus. He was what I call a proper comedian.'

'Ah, Ken Dodd. I saw him at Blackpool in the sixties. I always thought Knotty Ash was a made-up name until I met a Liverpudlian who actually came from there. I don't think the jam butty mines were real, though. I did like Billy Connolly, I have to admit. Mind you it took me some time to get used to his accent. One of my favourites was a joke he told on 'Parkinson'. 'Before you judge a man, walk a mile in his shoes. After that who cares? He's a mile away and you've got his shoes.' I seem to remember Parky was laughing so much he had a job to carry on with the interview.'

'Wasn't Connelly in a group called The Humblebums? Who was the singer who went on to become famous?'

'Gerry Rafferty. "Baker Street". I read somewhere that the sax player who did the famous riff was paid the standard session fee of £30. Raphael Ravenscroft I think it was. He didn't live far from here – from somewhere near Stoke. Bet he wished he'd asked for performance rights!'

'Back in the day we had the showbands in Ireland. They were really popular. Used to come over the border from the south. The first band I can remember going to see was "The Arrivals" in Dungannon. The place was heaving. All good fun. No alcohol because most of these dances were organised by the Catholic Church. Then there was "The Miami Showband". They were big. I saw them several times and got to know Steven Travers and Tony

Geraghty. "The Trixons" played several times locally – they were good as well. My friend was a farmer and several of us used to pile into the back of his Transit and he'd take us to the various gigs. I remember once he'd forgotten to clean it out after taking some pigs somewhere. We certainly cleared the dance floor that night.' Tommy sighed.

'Then it all came to an end. UVF set up a roadblock one night in County Down. 1975 I think it was. Stopped this minibus taking "The Miami Showband" back home to the south and shot and killed some of them. Rumour had it that some of the gunmen were army. After that the bands were too frightened to cross the border. Maybe the end was in sight anyway, what with the coming of discos. Good times, so they were.'

Batt and McCole continued on their way and five minutes later had arrived at the reservoir and parked behind the club house to unload their gear. They sat for a moment looking at the sailing boats at the top end of the water, and listening to the clinking of the rigging of the boats still waiting to be taken out.

'Reminds me of Lough Neagh when I was a youngster. My Da used to take me up there for the day. Course it was a lot bigger but it had the same peaceful feel. I think it helped Da unwind and forget about The Troubles which were kicking off again.'

'Was he involved in things?'

'Not in the violence. To be sure he took part in the occasional peaceful protest up in Belfast. As you know, that's how he met his end.'

Batt nodded and opened the boot.

'Grab the food and drink and I'll bring the rods,' he said. 'We need to sign in at the reception.'

A few minutes later they were in the boat and chugging under the causeway when his phone rang. It was a text from Baz to say DI Mills was in trouble with the Chief for demolishing Ben Rogers' door.

When he looked up Tommy was smiling.

'What's so funny?' asked Batt.

'Oh nothing really. Isn't technology a marvellous thing?'

'Aye, when it works.'

'I was just thinking how useful a mobile phone would have been when I was in Limerick Jail. Back in the day we had to roll messages up into a ball, wrap them in clingfilm, and pass them from mouth to mouth with our loved ones when they came to visit if we wanted to contact someone on the outside.'

Batt returned the grin.

'I hear they use drones now to deliver drugs and things. Hover them outside a prisoner's window until he can grab whatever's tied to them.'

'So,' continued McCole, 'shall we stop all the shenanigins and lay our cards on the table? You know who I am and I've a pretty shrewd idea who you are.'

Batt continued to set up their lines, thinking how best to respond.

'Go on,' he said.

'You know, looking back we all have things we regret doing.'

He took the opened bottle Batt was handing him.

'Slainte. Me, I've been responsible for taking the lives of innocent people – sons, daughters, mothers, fathers. It shouldn't have been like that. I always instructed my units to give warnings and plenty of time for areas to be cleared.

Not everyone in The Organisation was a thug – although you'd be hard pushed to justify some of the actions of the Newry brigade. I can think of one of our bombing team, Paddy Sheehy, who mistook a man breaking into his car in London for a member of MI5. He shot and killed the man and felt so bad about it that he eventually took his own life. I suppose all our units attracted their fair share of psychos, particularly amongst the rank and file, and we used them to take a no-holds-barred attitude towards the army and to a lesser extent the RUC. If you'd been on the receiving end of their brutality then you'd perhaps understand.

It kicked off with Bloody Sunday in January of seventy-two – thirteen of our people shot dead, including my da, during a peaceful civil rights march when we protested about internment. Do you know that no Protestants were interred? All Catholics. You hear about the Falls Road Curfew later the same year? Five Catholics were murdered, many of us were beaten up, and our homes were ransacked. Our furniture was smashed and thrown out onto the streets. Can you believe the army even smashed our crucifixes?

We retaliated with bombings and murders. In the same year as the Falls Road Curfew we were responsible for well over four hundred deaths, more than a hundred of them members of the armed forces.'

He paused to help Batt set up the fishing gear.

'So, for as long as the UK government seemed happy to let it continue on our home soil it was obvious we needed to bring the disruption closer to home. I was moved to the mainland in the late seventies to oversee the bombing campaign there. You have to believe me, George, my units were always instructed to give plenty of warning when a bomb was about to go off. I still, to this day, don't know why some of those warnings weren't acted on.'

Batt looked at him but said nothing.

'Maurice Oldfield was Head of MI6 at the time, which is why I was sent to live in Derbyshire. His family had a farm in Youlgreave. 'Meadow Place' it was called. I remember it well. Lovely setting in the Derbyshire dales, looking out over Lathkill Dale. Not one of your landed gentry type of farm. Quite a modest place, really. Oldfield often visited. I don't think he liked London much. He played the organ, you know – even played it at his local church. Must have driven his security team mad. About the only precaution he took was to install one of his officers, Diane Phillips, in the Royal Oak pub to keep an eye on any strangers. It was me who built the bomb we planted under his car. We gave them a warning, of course, and the army made it safe.

This was before we used Kim Philby and his son Tommy to get us Semtex from Russia, and before we developed remote controlled detonations using camera flashes and mobile phones.

I supplied gelignite that had been brought in from America and the old fashioned type of timer to make it easy for them. Same with the bomb that was hung on the railings outside his London home. If that one had gone up it would have blown the feathers off his chickens in Youlgreave. Biggest bomb ever found in this country in peacetime. But we were making a point, you see. We had the ability to kill the top people if we chose to.

Maurice retired in 1980 and died the next year. He was a good man. Brought a bit of calm to the situation.'

'So,' said Batt, 'you regret what you've done?'

'Not so much what I've done as having to do it. Do you know, George, there were too many lives lost during the thirty years of The Troubles, but there have been more suicides since then as a legacy of The Toubles than there were murders during those thirty years. I think that fact was raised in Parliament recently during Prime Ministers Questions.'

'So what exactly was your role in England, Tommy?'

'Procurement was one. Organisation was the other. A courier would bring over money and instructions. I got hold of whatever was needed for a job and organised a team to work with the planner to carry it out.'

'So you knew who actually carried out an act?'

'No, not always. I knew the names of all our mainland operatives but when a planner asked for support I used a random selection method based on coded numbers to pair a bomb maker with a planter, or a driver with a shooter so I never actually knew who had done what. Basic security. If I or one of the team was caught we wouldn't know the names of the others.

'What other things were you involved in?'

'Nothing major – at least, not that I'm aware of. About the same time as Oldfield's death the Brits employed the so-called supergrass tactic. You heard of it?'

Batt shook his head and took a bite from his cake.

'The Brits set up a huge fund to pay informers to give them our names. Two IRA grasses, McWilliams and Kennedy got sixteen of us put away just on the strength of their word. I don't know what happened to the pair of them. I do know they were given new homes, new identities and new faces. We reckoned nearly thirty of our men were tempted by the money. We executed six of them and kneecapped a good few others. They'd all known about the death sentence in the Green Book so it serves them right.'

'The Green Book? Wasn't that the IRA's handbook?'

'It was that. It set out all our strategies and thinkings behind the purpose of the bombing campaigns and the use of propoganda. It also gave advice about what to expect from the army if captured and interrogated. I can still remember the words: 'say nothing, sign nothing, see nothing, hear nothing'. And, as I say, the book also included sanctions you could expect if you violated our code - the so-called death sentences. All new recruits were given a Green Book.'

'I seem to remember a copy falling into government hands when Seamus Twomey was captured.'

'It did, aye. One of the reasons we changed strategies in the late seventies.

Anyway, as a consequence of the supergrass policy, I was thought to be in danger and so McGuiness had me lie low. I did make a short comeback in 1990.

Remember Sir Peter Terry? He lived at a place called Milford Common near Stafford. He had been the Governor of Gibraltar and was responsible for Operation Flavious a couple of years earlier – the one where the SAS gunned down some of our men in cold blood. It turns out I made the bomb that nearly killed him. Oh, and the attack on Lichfield train station that same year. We sent in two armed men to frighten soldiers on their way back to Whittington Barracks. Unfortunately they went too far and one soldier was killed and two others wounded. Our lads escaped over the railway tracks and into a builder's yard where someone was waiting in a van for them.

I have to admit I was also involved in supplying for the hotel bombing campaign.

But that was the end, really. I was asked to do a bit of intelligence work from time to time, but not any active service;"

'So you weren't involved in the Harrods bombing or the Brighton bombing?'

'Only in the sense of procurement. Direct involvement was really above my pay grade. Shortly after that campaign I was ordered to stand down because the security forces had me under observation.'

Batt stared at him.

'Our long term goal was a political solution to the Troubles. I'm not trying to make excuses for what I was involved in but the bombings and the shootings seemed the only way at the time to persuade your government to sit down and talk with us.

And Thatcher's people did sit down with us, behind closed doors that is. Both sides recognised that, in time, we Catholics would outnumber the Prods and that, come a

General Election, Sinn Fein would eventually win more seats in the Province than anyone else.

And it's now happened, although our MPs still refuse to sit in the House.

Do you know, George, by the time I was deployed on the mainland in the late seventies, working-age Catholics were one third of the population and yet we made up nearly seventy percent of the unemployment figures. At the same time, there were more Catholic children that Prods. Well those kids are adults now and there are more of us of a voting age that the other lot. That's why we now control Stormont. And that's why money will finally be used to improve employment, housing and schools in Catholic ghettos.

We only ever wanted equality and when we finally get it the likes of me won't be needed.'

There was silence, just the sound of a few water birds calling to one another from the reeds.

'Quite a speech,' said Batt, after a while.

'Och, I do have my occasional moments of clarity you know.'

'How bad is the dementia?'

'It's vascular dementia – not to be confused with Alzheimer's. Apparently the blood vessels in my brain are getting restricted, stopping messages from getting through. Sometimes the flow is OK and sometimes it's too slow. Eventually, so they tell me, it'll get to the stage where some of the vessels get permanently blocked, in my case starting with the ones that control my short term memory and then progressing to my medium term memory.

Kind of ironic, don't you think? I want to forget about the past and sometimes it's the only thing I can remember. Hopefully I'll die of a brain hemorrhage before that happens. Not a nice way to go but who wants to end up like some of the poor souls in the Home?'

'Best make sure you've had a priest give you the last rites before you go, after what you've done in this life.'

'True. Although I've already sought absolution. The Sacrament of Penance is a marvellous thing. You should try it some time.'

'I doubt my God is as forgiving as yours.

Come on, let's move over to the other side of the water for twenty minutes and see if we have any more luck with the fish.'

They stowed their rods, Batt started up the motor and McCole guided them towards a plantation of fir trees, their reflection creating a mirror image in the still water. In the distance several people could be seen walking, most with dogs in tow. One couple was sat near the water's edge enjoying a picnic. A child came running out of the woods towards them. She stopped dead in her tracks when she saw the motor launch. The woman offered her a drink and said something. The toddler looked across to Batt and McCole and waved.

McCole waved back and shouted, 'We're pirates and we're looking for buried treasure. Have you seen any?'

The girl laughed and pointed towards the trees before sitting down on the rug and helping herself to a sandwich from a tin.

'We ought to do the same,' said Batt, reaching for the lunch box. He'd seen McCole's face soften when talking to the child.

'You ever married,' he asked.

McCole reached over and took a sausage roll.

'Only to The Cause,' came the reply. 'She was a tough mistress but I had a deep love for her. 'First we feel and then we fall'. James Joyce,' he added. "I felt the injustice and I fell for the way of revenge.'

He seemed lost in thought, chewing slowly. He sighed and looked at Batt.

' Don't grow old and have any regrets, George. Life isn't a rehearsal, as they say. What about you?'

'I was married. Would have been thirty years this August just gone.'

'What happened?'

'Cancer happened. Treatment came to a halt during Covid. She was halfway through a new type of treatment – a stem cell transplant. I remember sitting with her in the chemo ward at Birmingham after they had been harvested, watching the nurses carefully package her stem cells in ice. Then a motorcycle volunteer came and took them away. It was quite emotional, knowing it was perhaps her only hope. They had to be transported to a lab in America to be modified. For some reason the British airport authorities wouldn't allow them to be transported from here and so a team of volunteer riders took them all the way to Amsterdam. Can you imagine? All that way for someone you didn't know.'

'But it didn't work?' asked Tommy.

'The lab modified the cells and sent them back. Unfortunately the government suddenly took the decision to close all the cancer wards. The consultant was in tears when he broke the news to us. His team was being redeployed to Covid wards.

Anyway, the stem cells were deep frozen and stored but by the time they could be used she was too ill for the transplant to work. She died in my arms at home.'

'I'm sorry,' said McCole. 'Seems we've both been denied, one way or the other.'

He looked up and saw Batt wipe away a tear.

'You still find it hard?'

'I cry most days, Tommy. Sometimes for her, sometimes for me but usually for the both of us.'

'Ay, losing someone is hard. I lost my family when I moved over here. And more,' he added. 'So much more.'

They continued eating in silence until Batt gave a shout. McCole ducked instinctively as Batt jumped over his legs and dived to the other side of the boat.

'Got one,' he yelled. 'Pass me the landing net, Tommy'

'For the love of God,' said McCole. 'I thought you were shouting a warning.'

He picked himself up from the bottom of the boat.

'Here I'll give you a hand.'

He watched as Batt expertly played the fish in and deftly swung it into the net he was holding over the side of the boat. He removed the hook and dropped fish and net back over the side.

'Perch,' said McCole. 'Not a bad size.'

He watched the fish as it circled just under the water, the orange fins flicking this way and that.

'That's your supper sorted. We'll ask cook to pan fry it in butter. Full of vitamins. You'll feel like a new man in the morning.'

McCole laughed and passed him an apple.

'But you haven't brought me all the ways out here just to catch me some supper. What is it you want, George?'

Batt baited the line again and cast towards the bank.

'A Kieran Wells was found dead in his flat not far from here a few days ago. Seems, from what I've been told, that he had got himself into a spot of bother during the seventies over in Belfast and had to be smuggled out by the security forces. He'd been living under a false name and a new identity. An old friend of yours thought you might be able to help us find his killer.'

'And what will you do if you do find him?'

'Me? I personally won't be doing anything. I've just been tasked with finding out who he – or she – is. My guess about what happens then is that it depends who this person is and why Wells was murdered. MI5 doesn't want to see any flare up of the old troubles, not now a peaceful solution might be in sight.'

'The name doesn't mean anything. Probably borrowed from someone who would have been about the same age but who died young. Anything you can tell me about him? Description, identifying marks?'

Batt gave what information he could about the man, concluding, 'Dental work wasn't British but shrapnel found in his abdomen was.'

'And how did he die, George?'

'Seems like it was an overdose of sodium pentothal. He was then shot in the head at close range to make it look like that was the cause of death.'

McCole looked thoughtful.

'We were supplied sodium pentothal in the seventies by the Russians. That supply dried up after a short while. It was volatile stuff. You had to know just how much to administer to get results. Too much and your subject died before you could get anything out of him. What about the mortar fragments?'

'They were from an experimental type of alloy only used by the British army in the Province. This narrows down the time he was serving there. My understanding is it must have been between 1974 and 1976.'

McCole thought hard.

'McWilliams and Kennedy were ghosted out at about that time. One or two others also disappeared from the scene, but probably on the orders of our Chiefs of Staff. What makes you think we're responsible for the death of this Kieran Wells in any case?'

'He was a double agent. Reached a pretty senior position in the IRA, or so I'm told.'

Tommy looked visibly shaken. He stared hard at Batt.

'I'll need time to check some things out. I think our fishing expedition has been just that. Shall we call it a day?'

He rubbed his forehead.

'You OK Tommy?'

'Bit of a headache coming on. I seem to get them quite often. Probably having to listen to that lot all the time at Mount View.

Anyway I've got homework to do and it's due in tomorrow.'

'Homework, Tommy?'

'Yes, Colm. For Sister Bridgette. You know what she's like if you haven't done it. My knuckles are still sore from the last time.'

Batt nodded, packed away their gear and started up the motor. They headed for the launch ramp in silence, Tommy sitting in the stern looking for all the world like Finlay Currie's Magwich from the 1946 film "Great Expectations".

Chapter 9

Batt had been making use of the last of his two days off by catching up on some jobs around the house. He had weeded the path, trimmed some bushes and treated his workshop with preservative. The house had had a long overdue clean from top to bottom. After a street run, he'd spent the evening relaxing by listening to some Harvey Andrews whilst reassembling a clock movement he'd been restoring. By eight-thirty he had decided to call it a day and get ready for a night shift.

It took him longer than normal to get to Mount View. He turned off the main road and onto the country lane and was approaching the bend when a tractor cam hurtling round the corner and shuddered to a halt a few feet from his bonnet. It was pulling a trailer of what looked like grain. Batt sighed and started to reverse back to the junction. Reversing was not something that came naturally to him, and reversing in the fading light was something he could have done without. When he eventually got back to the main road he waited for the tractor to edge past but when it drew level he could see the driver with mobile phone in hand bending down to say something to him. He expected a critique on his lack of driving skills. He sighed and wound his window down.

'Thanks Bud. That car's been parked in the passing place all day. It's not the first time, either. Blooming hiker or dog walker I expect. Have they no sense? I'd a good mind to give it a scrape when I drove past. I'm sick of it. Idiots are always parking in this passing place. Anyway I've got his number so if it happens again I'll report him.'

'Getting the grain in?' Batt asked, hoping a change of subject might improve his mood.

'Aye. First of the spring barley. It's going to the local brewery. Not been a good year – too wet early on. I'll probably make a loss and with no subsidy now we've Brexited I shall be struggling. Anyway I'd best be off. They'll be waiting for me.'

He rammed the tractor into gear and moved off.

'What are the odds,' wondered Batt as he set off again, 'of coming across a farmer who was happy.'

He'd just parked up when Mount View's main door opened and, in the pool of light he saw Maria come hurrying towards him.

Batt jumped out and asked if everything was OK.

'George, it's Tommy. He is very poorly. I send for ambulance.'

Batt led her inside and asked what had happened.

'Miriana heard alarm go off in Tommy's room and Tommy shouting for help. When she got there he was lying on the floor in a lot of pain and hitting his head with his hands. Now he not breathing much.'

They hurried down the corridor. They stopped at Tommy's open doorway. Batt could see two care staff kneeling on the floor beside Tommy.

'It is such a shame, George. He was OK when cousin came again this afternoon but when he gone Tommy get very agitated. Kate said to watch for him because it was sign of big stroke coming.'

Batt was silent for a moment, watching one of the staff gently stroke Tommy's forehead.

'Did you speak to his cousin Maria?'

'Yes. I open door for him. He was very nice. He brought big box of biscuits for staff and present for Tommy. He say he is going back to Ireland in morning. He thank everyone for looking after Tommy.'

'What time would this have been?'

'I go check visitors' book for you.'

Batt was aware of a blue circling light outside and heard the main door being opened. Maria pointed two young paramedics in his direction and stood back to let them enter. One of them was already removing things from her backpack and, after a brief discussion the other left the room and headed back outside. He returned a few moments later wheeling a gurney.

Maria joined him again and the pair of them watched as Tommy's body was gently placed on it. As they made their way past, Batt raised a questioning eyebrow to one of the ambulance crew. It was answered by a shake of the head. The two care staff followed them up the corridor.

Maria saw the look on Batt's face.

'I'm so sorry, George. I know we shouldn't get attached to residents...'

'But we're only human,' he concluded.

She squeezed his arm and said, 'I go to check what time cousin arrive.'

Left on his own, he surveyed the room. A bedside cabinet had been moved, presumably by the paramedics, and on the floor where Tommy had lain were a few empty boxes of things they had used to try to save him.

He moved into the room and looked round. Nothing seemed out of place. On the chest of drawers was Tommy's camera and propped up against a pile of books was a photograph that he hadn't seen before. He picked it up and studied it. It was of a couple. The young man was unmistakably Tommy. He was standing hand in hand with a pretty dark-haired girl who was smiling up at him, both very much in love. They were standing in front of a shop window advertising Cookstown sausages. He flicked the photograph over and read the words "I love you" written in neat female handwriting.

'Yes,' he thought, 'You were right, Tommy. You certainly lost more than just family to The Cause.'

Replacing the picture was when he noticed it: a small ball of paper wrapped in cling film. He picked it up and put it in his pocket. Then he checked the camera. The memory card had been removed.

He looked up to see Maria standing in the doorway. He went across, turned to look at the empty room, and quietly closed the door.

'Tommy's cousin Brendan arrive at just after four,' she said.

'Brendan?'

'Yes. He sign in as Brendan Quinn.'

'Did you see him out when he left?'

'No. I very busy helping get tea served. It very busy time for everyone. I don't think he sign out.'

Batt considered things for a moment. This cousin had arrived just before tea was served, probably knowing it was a time the staff would be preoccupied. If he'd let himself out how had he managed it without knowing the door lock's combination and where to find the switch to turn off the alarm? Batt's time serving in Afghanistan had taught him not to believe in coincidences. This cousin – someone who Tommy says couldn't have known where to find him - arrives at a busy time, is not seen leaving by anyone, and later that evening Tommy dies.

Before he could question Maria further there was a scream and the sound of crashing coming from the kitchen.

Batt took off in that direction and found the cook lying on the floor in a pool of water. Freshly peeled potatoes were scattered all over the place. She was uttering an impressive range of expletives. He moved a half empty potato sack out of the way and knelt down beside the dazed woman.

'I'm alright, George. Really. I just need a moment to gather myself. Can you help me up?'

'Are you sure nothing's broken?'

'No. I've just got a bruised ego.'

'Is that a euphamism?'

'Very funny. Come on. Give me a hand up.'

George got her sitting on a stool. She rubbed he arm vigorously.

'So what happened?'

'No idea. One minute I'm peeling the spuds for tomorrow's dinner and the next thing I know they're fighting back. I must have tripped on that sack and knocked the pan off the worktop as I went down.'

Maria arrived and made suitably sympathetic noises whilst Batt started to clear up the mess. He collected as many King Edwards as he could find and asked where the mop was kept.

'In the tall cupboard over by the door,' he was told.

He made his way over and noticed the outside door wasn't closed properly.

'Mandy, has anyone been outside recently?'

Mandy turned round on her stool.

'Sometimes the staff sneak out for a fag but I don't remember anyone doing that tonight, and I've been here since eight.'

Batt opened the door and peered out. The ambulance was trundling slowly down the drive and the two carers were just going back inside.

Suddenly a figure ran from behind the workshops, across the car park and disappeared into the shadows of a clump of trees on the edge of the grounds. Batt took off after him. When he got to the fence he climbed on a rail and stood listening whilst his eyes adjusted to the darkness. He didn't have to move but whoever he was following did. He heard nothing out of the ordinary. Where was he heading?

And then it dawned on him. Out here in the middle of nowhere meant whoever it was must have come by car and left it nearby. The passing place.

He moved through the trees in the direction of the lane and joined it not far from the bend where he had encountered the tractor. He moved carefully, keeping as close to the hedgerow as possible. He could see the car a short distance ahead. He dropped down into the ditch and waited. Nothing happened. An owl hooted and from the main road came the occasional muffled sound of a car. After five minutes he decided to risk moving closer. He climbed onto the lane and slowly made his way forwards.

Suddenly the car's headlights lit up and blinded him. He instinctively put up his arm to shield his eyes at the same time as he heard the engine burst into life. The car shot forwards in a spray of stones and mud. Batt took off to his left and felt the impact as the front wing made contact with his back. He lay on the verge in a heap, winded. His back felt like it was on fire.

Looking up he saw the reversing lights come on and the vehicle shoot backwards towards him. He half crawled, half rolled into the ditch moments before he would have been hit again. The car took off down the lane, it's tail lights disappearing round the bend. This time it kept going.

In the silence that followed Batt lay where he was for a while, unable and unwilling to move. Eventually he sat up and propped himself against the side of the ditch before crawling out onto the verge. He could feel a wet patch at the side of his head but it felt like mud rather than blood. The same with both legs. His back was beginning to throb, though. In the circumstances he considered he'd got off lightly. He carefully raised himself to his feet and began to retrace his steps.

A now-recovered Mandy let him in through the kitchen door., took one look at him and let out a gasp.

'George! Whatever happened? Are you all right? Should I call an ambulance?'

She guided him over to a chair and sat him down before running into the corridor to summon help. It was Miriana who was the first to arrive, followed soon after by Maria who had been getting ready to leave.

Batt looked up at the three concerned faces.

'It's not as bad as it looks. When I went to look for a mop to help clean up after Mandy's fall, I noticed the outside door wasn't closed properly. When I looked out I thought I saw someone hiding by the trees. My first thought was that Wilf had got out when the ambulance was here for Tommy so I ran over but couldn't see anyone. I heard a noise and assumed he'd climbed the fence and was heading for the lane. I thought I'd better follow him but when I came out of the woods and into a field I found myself surrounded by cows. I panicked and tried to push them out of the way but it must have spooked them and before I knew it I'd been knocked to the ground and trampled on.'

He could see they were too concerned about the state he was in to question his story.

'Is Wilf missing?' he asked, hoping to move further talk away from himself.

'I checked on him about half an hour ago,' said Miriana, 'and he was fast asleep. His bed alarm hasn't gone off but I'll go and make sure he's still there.'

She disappeared, leaving Maria and Mandy to fuss over him.

Maria said, 'Do you want me to call Kate and ask her to come so you can go home?'

'I'll be fine, Maria. I'm just a bit sore.'

'What, around your ego?' said Mandy, and laughed. 'But you can't carry on working looking like that. We keep spare sets of clothes for the residents in case they need them. I not sure we have any your size but I go look. Why don't you get shower and I leave clothes by door. I stay until you done, then I go home. No hurry.'

Batt did as he was told, passing Miriana in the corridor who smiled and gave him the thumbs up. Evidently the resident Houdini was still enjoying his beauty sleep.

He emerged a few minutes later, dressed in brown corduroy trousers that were far too short, and a pink polo neck jumper that would probably have fitted him better when he was a child. Still, beggars couldn't be choosers. He was grateful no-one laughed at him, at least not to his face. He put his own clothes in a pile by the door.

Maria left, telling them she would see them tomorrow, and Miriana asked Batt if he would mind helping to clear Tommy's room.

She must have seen the look he gave her because she explained, 'It seems a bit disrespectful I know, George, but we have to keep all the rooms occupied or we lose money. We have fee payers waiting to come and private fee payers are worth a lot more than council funded ones. To be honest it's the private residents that subsidise the local authority ones. If we can get the room cleared tonight we can get somebody new in tomorrow.'

'I understand,' said Batt. What do you want me to do?'

'Just put Tommy's personal belongings into a cardboard box, strip the bed and I will get someone to clean the room. I better check on the residents again but if you need anything just give me a shout.'

Batt took the box he was offered and went back to Tommy's room. He was beginning to stiffen up. A bit of moving around would help.

He started in the bathroom and gathered up Tommy's comb, razor, toothbrush and deodorant. Back in the bedroom he emptied the drawers of the few clothes that were in them. In one of them he found a wallet containing a bank card and an out-of-date driving licence, plus a few coins in a zipped compartment. Using his phone, he photographed the card and licence before picking up the photograph. Would anyone know it was missing if he kept it? He thought not so he slipped it into the back pocket of his trousers. Apart from those few things there was nothing else to pack. He put the box near the door and stripped the bed before going off to find Miriana again.

She was speaking to another staff member so he waited until she'd finished.

'How are you feeling George?'

Batt smiled. 'I'll survive. Miriana, what will the funeral arrangements be for Tommy?'

'You were fond of him weren't you. He seemed lost until you arrived on the scene. You were good for him. I'm not sure what the arrangements will be. Cremation I would think. Kate will know whether he has left a will but I don't think he was in touch with any family. Except for the cousin who was here today, but he said he was going home to Ireland and we haven't any means of getting in touch with him.'

'Well, I was thinking. Could you could print me his picture from the CCTV recording? Maria says he arrived at just gone four. I have a friend in the police who could put out an alert for him in case he hasn't left yet. It's worth a try, surely?'

'I'm not sure how to do that.'

'I can give you a hand.'

They went to the manager's office and Miriana sat in front of the monitor with Batt looking over her shoulder. He guided her through the process of selecting the main entrance's camera, and through to the time when Tommy's cousin had arrived. He could be seen walking up the drive with a couple of gift-wrapped parcels in his hand. As the figure approached the door Batt leant over and pressed the pause button. He was looking at a man of average height who was probably in his fifties, wearing casual trousers and an open-necked shirt. Batt moved the footage on to the moment Tommy's cousin looked up to ring the door bell. His face looked drawn and tired but, like the rest of him, was fairly unremarkable. He had, Batt noticed, an earring in his left ear.

He explained to Miriana how to improve the picture's quality and resolution.

'We need a memory stick to transfer the image to a computer so we can print it out. Any idea where Kate might keep one?'

'No. But I know where there is one – in the CD player in the lounge. We record the music on it that we play to the residents. I'll go and fetch it.'

She got up leaving Batt to study the face on the monitor.

She was soon back and watched as Batt did what was necessary to capture the image. He fired up Kate's PC and soon the printer began to chug out the picture.

Batt sat back and looked at the result. It wasn't brilliant but hopefully good enough for what he had in mind. He deleted the image from the memory stick and handed it back to Miriana. Then he shut down the computer and stood up. His back was throbbing.

'I hope your friend in the police can find Tommy's cousin. Everyone deserves a proper funeral.'

She gave him a look of appraisal.

'You look a bit the worse for wear. Is this the first time you've been on the night shift?'

Batt nodded.

'I'd normally ask you to keep a check on the residents on the top corridor until about five o'-clock and then start to help with getting the breakfast things ready before the next shift arrive at six. I'll tell you what, though. You stay here and monitor the CCTV of the corridors and check the panel for any alerts, and I'll go upstairs and do the rounds.'

'That's very kind. I must say I'm a bit shaken up.'

'Right. Before I forget, you need to fill in the accident book. And can you catch cook before she clocks off and ask her to do the same?'

'Will do,' said Batt. 'And thanks.'

Left on his own in the office he did a quick inventory of the shelf full of files. He pulled out the one marked "Residents' Information" and quickly found the page for Tommy. It contained details of not only his bank account but his date of birth, date of admission and things like medical conditions. Of the two phones in his pocket, he took out O'Brien's and photographed the sheet along with the print-out of Quinn's image.

He was about to forward it to O'Brien when he heard footsteps approaching. He quickly put the file back on the shelf and the phone into his trouser pocket.

The footsteps continued down the corridor. Probably one of the staff off to the kitchen for their break.

He sat thinking about what his next move should be. In theory his time at Mount View was over now that Tommy McCole was dead. He wondered how O'Brien would want to play it. If he had to leave he'd be sorry. He'd grown attached to both the residents and the staff.

He decided the first thing he would do was find out the registration number of the car that had been parked in the lane. With any luck it might have been captured on his dash cam but if not then he would have to track down the farmer and come up with an excuse for asking him. O'Brien and his team at MI5 might be able to have the vehicle tracked using motorway surveillance cameras and the like.

He also thought it might be an idea to ask Siobhan if she knew the pathologist at Stoke, which was where Tommy's body had been taken. He'd like to know the cause of death and whether there was any chance it had been a copy-cat of Kieran Wells's.

Then there was the rolled up ball of paper wrapped in clingfilm that he'd taken from Tommy's room. He subconsciously checked his trouser pocket to make sure it was still there. There was obviously something important contained in it, something that Tommy knew he had to pass on to Batt before it was too late. He realised he hadn't come across any used wrapping paper when he'd cleared the room. Quinn must have taken Tommy's present with him when he left.

Where to start? He would finish his shift at six in about a couple of hours. Farmers always got up early, especially if they had grain to get in before the weather turned. Thunder storms had been forecast for later in the week. He'd start by making a trip to the brewery.

Time passed slowly and Batt was conscious that whoever was responsible for nearly killing him was probably well on his way to catching the early morning ferry to Ireland. He thought about contacting O'Brien but before he could do so a red light flashed on the monitoring board. He checked the CCTV images on the screen but all seemed quiet in the corridor outside room seventeen. He paged Miriana to let her know. A few minutes later she got back to him with the news that it was Elsie and that she'd got the trots. Could Batt change her sheets whilst Miriana saw to Elsie?

By the time he'd finished and taken the soiled things to the laundry room, it was beginning to get light. He heard a couple of cars draw up into the car park as the next shift started to arrive.

On the stroke of six he went to collect his clothes from the kitchen. The air was already full of the smells of breakfast and several staff sitting around a table enjoying toast and coffee whilst waiting for Miriana to brief them at handover. They turned to look at Batt.

One of them called out, 'Morning George. I don't know what they've been feeding you overnight but you seem to have outgrown your clothes.'

Batt looked down at his ill-fitting attire. 'It's a bit of a long story. I found out I'm not a cow whisperer.'

They looked baffled.

'You'll have to wait for handover to find out. Got to go. Have a good shift.'

He grabbed a piece of toast that seemed to be going spare and made his way out to his car.

The first thing he did was to check his dash cam footage. When he'd rewound to the recording of the passing point he could just about make out what looked like a grey family hatchback – it could have been a Kia or perhaps a Toyota – but before the car's registration number had come into view the footage disintegrated into a flash of white as the tractor's headlights had speared the darkness from around the corner. He replayed it and pressed pause in an effort to see if he could make out anything else about the parked car but there was nothing. He was going to have to find the farmer who said he'd taken the vehicle's details.

He got them sooner than he had expected. He was heading back towards the main road when the tractor appeared pulling an empty trailer. Batt flashed his lights and began to reverse towards the passing place. This time it was Batt's turn to lean out of his window and signal to the farmer that he wanted a word.

'Morning. About the car that has been parking here. I work at Mount View and one of the staff thinks she might know who it belongs to. Have you still got the registration number?'

'Yes Bud, it's on my phone. Hang on a minute and I'll find it.'

He reached across the cab, picked up his mobile and soon gave Batt the details.

'If it is who your mate thinks it is then tell him from me that if he parks here again I'll use me forklift attachment and dump his car over the other side of the hedge.'

He didn't wait for any response before roaring off.
'Still no happier,' thought Batt.

Chapter 10

He did not have a particularly comfortable sleep. When his alarm woke him at eleven in the morning he almost had to roll out of his bed and onto the carpet. He attempted to stand but couldn't straighten up properly. He did a sort of crawl across the floor, over the landing and into the bathroom where he managed to raise himself up enough to be able to use the toilet. At least there was no sign of blood so his kidneys seemed to have survived the impact with the car's bonnet. He moved ape-like over to the bath and ran some water. Climbing in was painful; climbing out again five minutes later was less so. He got dressed, did some stretching exercises, took a couple of Paracetamol and made his way slowly down the stairs.

'Mr O'Brien, it's George. I think we need to chat. Tommy McCole is dead.'

'Suspicious circumstances?' asked O'Brien's voice down the phone.

'Hard to say what caused his death, but if you can track down a vehicle and its driver then you might have found Kieran Wells's killer as well.'

He gave O'Brien the details.

'Said he was Tommy's cousin over here on business. Signed the visitors' book as a Brendan Quinn. He was obviously determined to find something out from Tommy. I don't know if he used sodium pentothal like he did with Kieran Wells – always assuming the two deaths are linked – but we'll find out from the path. report. Could take a few days, though.'

'Leave it with me, George. I'll set about getting the car found. What do you think this Brendan Quinn is after?'

'You said there were two British agents who had infiltrated the IRA's central command. Tommy told me about two high-ups who suddenly disappeared off the radar. McWilliams and Kennedy. He reckoned they were responsible for the deaths of several IRA men. Maybe Dunne was close to one of them and is out for revenge. Or maybe, as you feared, it's one of the terrorist groups beginning a mopping-up operation. Was Wells one of the two British agents? In which case "yer man" is probably looking for the other.'

There was silence from O'Brien's end before he said, 'Let's hope, if that's the case, that he's on a personal mission and not one of a unit that's been assigned to carry out revenge killings. The repercussions of a new wave of violence would have an enormous impact on power sharing and Stormont. Either way he's got to be stopped. I'll be in touch. Keep this phone on.'

'Will do.'

Batt ended the call and went upstairs to run himself another bath in an attempt to ease the pounding in his back. Through the mirror he could see the beginnings of a sizeable bruise and knew he'd be as stiff as a board unless he kept moving.

He soaked for a few minutes, got dressed and retrieved Tommy's balled-up message before putting on a wash-load. The day was already warm and sticky. It seemed like the storms were coming sooner than expected. His new farming friend would not be happy. He wondered just how much barley he had left to get in.

He made himself some breakfast and went outside to eat it. He could hear the sound of several lawnmowers as people took advantage of the last day of dry weather. Across the way the church clock struck nine and was followed shortly after by the sound of the hand bell coming from the village school, warning late-comers to get a move on.

He decided to phone Siabhan Fahy. Hopefully he'd catch her before she started the first of the day's autopsies. She answered on the third ring.

'Good morning George. You're interrupting coffee and a Hobnob so it better be important.'

Batt explained the events of the previous night.

'I was wondering where they would have taken Tommy.'

'Stoke General,' she replied.

'Know anyone there?'

'A pathologist, do you mean? Yes. Peter Mann. We trained together. Why?'

'I need to know whether Tommy died the same way as Kieran Wells – the body found at Fairview Mansions.'

'Sodium pentathol? I take it you may have established a link?'

'Not sure. But if that drug is present in Tommy McCole then it will confirm it.'

'Leave it with me. I'll get on to Stoke as soon as I've finished this Hobnob. Don't you wish you were into comfort eating, George?'

'My body is a temple, you know that.'

'Aye. An old ruined temple. Have a good day. I'll get back to you as soon as I can. By the way, have you treated that greenfly yet?'

She rang off and Batt got slowly to his feet to inspect his roses.

Most had been planted in containers and Fran had arranged them by the kitchen door. Now every time he opened it and breathed in their scent, memories of happier times came flooding back. She would never have allowed them to be neglected.

He walked down the path to the small potting shed where she had spent so much time. As he pulled the door open he pictured her standing there smiling, a glass of lemonade in one hand and a tray of seedlings in the other.

He looked round for some rose spray, saw her gardening gloves laid on the bench and, in a mix of anger and frustration, hurled a trowel at the wall opposite. He wondered whether his was a normal grieving process or whether he perhaps needed some help.

Then the phone O'Brien had given him rang.

'DI Batt? O'Brien here. We've motorway cameras looking out for the car. and I will soon have people in place to watch the ferry ports to Ireland. It's a Ford Mondeo, by the way. Plates are cloned, of course. The donor vehicle is registered to a lady living in the Birmingham area. She's a magistrate so I think we can safely rule her out. I'm sending a team to your neck of the woods just in case this Brendan Quinn is still in the area.'

O'Brien rang off before Batt had a chance to tell him about the CCTV image.

He gave up looking for something to spray onto the roses. He'd buy whatever was needed next time he was in town. His mind in any case was on Tommy's message. He'd put off reading it until he'd had time to consider things. It was clear Tommy had primed him that time on Blithfield Reservoir when he had described how IRA prisoners in internment had passed and received messages. The fact that he'd prepared the message before the arrival of his "cousin" meant he perhaps knew his time was about up.

But what did Tommy know that was so important? Was it the same thing that his killer had tried to get out of Kieran Wells? And had he succeeded? Foremost in his mind, though, was whether the message he was about to read had been written by Tommy or by Quinn. Quinn could be luring him into a trap.

He collected up his breakfast things and went back inside. Before retrieving the small paper ball from where he'd hidden it in the hood of one of his clocks, he locked the outside door.

He sat down at the kitchen table and carefully removed the clingfilm before starting to slowly straighten out the paper ball.

What he read convinced him it had been written by Tommy: *And then we fall. 53.1951/53-11-42 N; 1.772/1-46-29 W. Come and find me.*

'Come and find me'? In Batt's mind this put a different complexion on things. Perhaps the note was not so much an acceptance of imminent death as an indication that Tommy had hoped to somehow make his way to Monyash. But why? And how did he plan to get there? Was this Brendan Quinn going to take him? Anyhow, Tommy's death made it all seem irrelevant now.

He looked again at the message. He recognised the quote as the one Tommy had used that day they had spent fishing on Blithfield Reservoir. The figures he recognised as map coordinates.

Out of curiosity he fired up his laptop and entered the numbers into the search box.

Monyash Church in Derbyshire.

A further search revealed it to be St. Leonards: "twelfth century with later additions". It had a remarkably tall spire which could, apparently, be seen for miles around. And it looked to be isolated. The location made sense; it was an area Tommy would have been very familiar with. Batt thought the church and the village of Monyash looked like a pleasant place to spend an afternoon. He wondered if Siobhan would like a trip out sometime. They could maybe have lunch in nearby Bakewell. He would enjoy looking round the antique shops he'd heard were there. It might also be a way for him to say goodbye to Tommy. Despite their obvious differences, he had grown to like him.

Force of habit made him destroy the message and replace it with another one with different coordinates. He fired up his laptop and got the figures for Youlgreave

Church which was in the next village to Monyash. He tried to imitate Tommy's handwriting, and kept the message the same except for adding the words "*You know what to look for. You'll find it here."* and then went into the lounge and taped the note to the inside of a longcase clock door.

If Brendan Quinn came looking for whatever it was he was desperate to get his hands on then hopefully he would find it. Batt had little doubt that he would be next on Quinn's visiting card. Putting the coordinates on his phone meant he could navigate there quickly if the situation arose.

For now though he decided to tidy up and get his head down for a few hours.

Things didn't quite go according to plan. He'd been washing up at the kitchen sink when he heard his back gate being opened. Looking up, he could see Jack walking slowly down the path. He stopped to smell a rose before looking up and catching sight of Batt. He waved a piece of wood at him in greeting. Batt dried his hands and unlocked the door.

'Jack. Come in.'

'Thank you very much. I'll not keep you. I'm getting the bus to Burton to do a bit of shopping. Just a few bits, like. It gets me out of the house.' And then, remembering why he'd come, added, 'I've made you that pillar for your clock. Hope it's alright.'

He held it out and Batt inspected it.

'Jack, that's perfect. I don't know how you do it. What do I owe you?'

'Owe me? It didn't cost anything. I used a bit of oak from an old chair that's been lying around. It'll be well seasoned.'

'Come and have a quick look at where it's going to fit.'

He led him through to the lounge where a clock hood lay on the table. Batt offered up the new part.

'Look at that. It's perfect. You're a genius.'

'Thank you very much, ta thank you. Very kind George. I always wished I'd gone into joinery rather than become a school caretaker but in my day you had to take what job you could.'

He led a beaming Jack back outside.

'It's getting very muggy. Reckon we're in for a storm. Could do with some rain, mind.'

'Try telling that to the farmers. They're in a race against time to get their crops combined and the grain stowed whilst it's still dry. Come on, I'll walk you to the bus stop.'

They walked down the path, through the gate and out onto the lane.

'What time's the bus due?'

Jack looked at his watch.

'Seven minutes. If I miss this one I've to wait three hours for the next. Oh, meant to tell you – your roses have a touch of greenfly. Got anything for them?'

Batt shook his head.

'I was going to get something next time I went shopping.'

'Washing up liquid,' said Jack. 'Works a treat. Just use a sprayer and give them a good soaking.'

They joined a couple of elderly women at the bus stop and exchanged greetings.

'Well thanks again Jack. Let me know if there's anything I can do in return.'

'Aye, I will, thank you.'

Batt left him to discuss the weather with the women and retraced his steps. Ten minutes and a couple of Ibuprofen later and he was flat out on the settee.

He awoke feeling a little less sore. He made himself a light lunch and decided he ought to go and strim Fran's grave before the rain that had been forecast came. He changed into some old clothes, fitted the battery to the strimmer that was kept in the potting shed, and set off down the lane.

Bishops Bromley church was on the southern edge of the village, next to open land where, in medieval times, commoners like himself would have been allowed to graze geese. The bishops of Burton had apparently chosen this spot for the common land because it was marshy and of little use to them. It remained largely untouched and allowed a pleasant view across the fields, especially on am day such as this. Batt made his way past the imposing Georgian vicarage with its intricately-patterned brickwork, through the lychgate and into the church yard. He nodded to a couple he didn't recognise – probably visitors come to look at the horns in the church – and turned down the path which led to the grave.

He began by tidying up the pots of plants. The hot weather hadn't been kind to them, even though he'd watered them regularly. He clearly didn't have Fran's green fingers. Then he took the strimmer and cut a neat rectangle of grass around the grave before stooping to brush cuttings from the headstone. He moved on to do the same to several other graves belonging to villagers she would have known either as neighbours or fellow members of the church choir.

He propped the strimmer up against the last stone and went to sit on the nearby bench, enjoying the peace and the warmth. Before long he felt his eyes begin to close.

He suddenly became aware he'd been joined on the bench by an elderly lady who introduced herself as Mary.

'Good to meet you Mary. I'm George.'

'You look as if you've been busy,' she said, eying the grass cuttings that had stuck to his shoes and trousers."

'My wife's grave.'

She had a kindly face and looked at him knowingly. When she continued to look at him he felt compelled to tell her more.

'Died of cancer during the Covid epidemic.'

For the first time Batt found himself opening up to someone, telling this stranger things he'd never told anyone before. He told her about the mis-diagnosis, the postponed hospital appointments, the tearful consultant who had broken the news she had stage four cancer. He told her about the thousands of miles they had travelled to hospitals for treatment and of how she had suffered but never once complained. He told her about her final moments that still haunted him – how in her final moments he had held her hand and read to her from her favourite book and how she had raised her hand in a sort of farewell as her soul left her body. And how a few minutes later the laboured breathing had finally ceased and he was left alone and still felt left alone almost three years later.

He realised tears were running down his cheeks.

He felt embarrassed and apologised. He fumbled for a tissue and blew his nose.

'It still makes me angry, you know? I see elderly couples enjoying each other's love and friendship and I think, 'That should have been us. We should have been able to grow old together.''

For a moment there was silence and he was aware he was gripping the bench so tightly that his knuckles were white with the force.

Mary touched his arm. 'You can either be thankful for the time God gave you together, or angry for the time you have been denied. And anger is a destructive emotion, don't you think, George?

And your wife will never leave you. Part of her will have become part of you.'

'I dream about her a lot. She's taken over from my nightmares. I was in Afghanistan,' he added as a way of explanation.

Mary nodded. 'And what about her friends? Do you still keep in touch? Her friends will be mourning, too. It is through you they can still connect with her.'

'I hadn't really thought of it like that. I'm not very good at keeping in touch, I'm afraid.

And what about you,' asked Batt. 'What brings you here? Do you have a relative in the churchyard?'

She gazed out across the fields. 'In a manner of speaking.'

They sat together for a while longer, enjoying the warmth of the sun. Batt felt a sense of calm and before long his eyes closed once more. When he awoke, Mary had gone.

****

It had rained hard in the night. If it had thundered he hadn't heard it. He poured himself a glass of juice and checked his own phone. No messages but at least the battery showed nearly full power. Then he checked O'Brien's. 'Call me'.

He glanced at the time and decided it would have to wait until he was on his way to Mount View.

What O'Brien had to say surprised him.

'We got an alert on that vehicle you had an argument with. If it was heading to Ireland then it was going the long way round. It was pinged going northbound on the A50 and a little later at Ashbourne on the A515 . We haven't had eyes-on since. Nothing so far at any of the ferry terminals. We've got them all covered – Liverpool and Cairnryan in case he's heading to the North, Fishguard,

Holyhead and Pembroke if it's to Ireland. Maybe he was having to collect something en route, so there's still a chance we'll pick him up at one of the ferry ports later today unless he's ditched the Mondeo for something else.'

Batt asked if the ports had facial recognition systems in place for foot passengers.

'All except Holyhead and Pembroke. Why?'

'I've a picture of him taken from Mount View's CCTV footage. With a bit of enhancement it might be good enough to add to their databases.'

'Send it over.'

He rang off.

Batt gave his sore back a rub and took a sip of his juice. He closed his eyes and gave O'Brien's words some thought. If Brendan Quinn had indeed intended to take Tommy to Monyash then there might have been things in the area that he needed to collect before heading back to the Province.

He stood up and went over to his bookshelf for a road atlas. His suspicions were correct. The A515 was the road to Monyash.

The care home was readying itself for a new day. The sky had cleared and the weather once again looked promising. One of the carers was out in the gardens wiping the benches when Batt pulled into the car park. He recognised her as one of the two who had sat with Tommy until the ambulance arrived. She called to ask how he was.

'A bit sore Lulia. I plan to keep well away from Hilda and her broomstick today.'

'Hilda will be busy this morning. She is having her hair done. The hairdresser comes every Thursday.'

She went back to wiping the benches and Batt let himself in through the kitchen door. He was met by the smell of freshly baked bread. Cook was taking another batch out of the oven when she noticed him.

'Good timing, George. Grab a piece and help yourself to some butter. When it's cooled you can take it in to the dining room. How are you, by the way?'

Batt picked up a knife and buttered a roll.

'I'll live.'

He noticed the trolley with the teapots and mugs on it.

'Do you want these taking through whilst the bread cools?'

'Thanks. Kate wants us off to a prompt start today. The vicar and his handbell ringers are coming at 9:30. Should be fun. Oh and our entertainments manager has asked if you could be the caller for this afternoon's prize bingo.'

'Prize bingo?'

"Apparently first prize is a CD of the bell ringers. It's called "Campanologists R Us". Kate says second prize is probably two copies.'

Batt was still smiling when he bumped into Maria.

'Ah, George. I was just coming for that,' she said, pointing to the trolley. 'How are you feeling? I hear you argue with cows.'

Before he could reply she broke out into a huge grin.

'George, I have news. My son he come to study at Birmingham. My husband he will drive him here and stay for a few days.'

'That's lovely news. What is your son going to study?'

'I think it is something to do with engineering. He is being sponsored by a big company in Romania - Kreftlanlagen. He only hear yesterday. I am so excited. You must meet my son and husband. We have meal together?'

'I'd like nothing better. I will look forward to it. But on one condition.'

Maria looked anxious.

'No garlic,' said Batt.

'Oh George. You had me worried. No garlic, I promise.'

'Here, you take the trolley in and I'll go and get the bread rolls.'

A little later that morning the residents had been rounded up and ushered into the lounge. Several were dozing in their chairs whilst others were chatting or reading. One or two family members were also present. Kate entered and mouthed 'OK?' to Batt who nodded in reply.

'Good morning everyone. I'd like to introduce our new resident, Sheila James.'

Sheila James was an immaculately dressed petite lady who smiled and nodded to the room in general. Batt noticed she was sitting in Tommy's chair. Everyone, it seemed, had their own place in the lounge.

'This morning we are very lucky to have the Marchington Bell Ringers coming to join us so let's settle down to listen to some lovely music.'

This was not exactly greeted with wild enthusiasm and Batt heard Hilda tell the room in general that she was sorry but unfortunately she wouldn't be there because she had a hair appointment, and then spoilt the moment by adding she hoped everyone had saved some of their breakfast bread rolls to stuff in their ears.

At 9:30 precisely the door bell chimed and out in the corridor the ringers could be heard assembling. They trooped in, dressed in blue crimpoline, and lined up behind row of tables upon which they placed their bells. The majority looked old enough to have been residents themselves. Batt half wondered whether they would be met on their way out by Kate handing them Mount View brochures .

The vicar said a few words of encouragement to his group, possibly offered up a prayer, and turned to address his captive audience.

'Good morning everyone. I'm the Reverend Lynton and the Marchington Bell Ringers and I have been looking forward to playing a few well-known tunes for you.'

When he got no response he turned back to the ringers and assumed the role of conductor.

They began with "Three Blind Mice" and ended half-an-hour later with "The Old Rugged Cross". The staff dutifully applauded and new resident Sheila thanked them as they made their way out. Batt breathed a sigh of relief that there had been no major incidents.

His own spot in the limelight came after dinner. Bingo cards were given to those who deemed capable of playing and the tea trolley was wheeled in displaying a selection of prizes. He was amused to see a copy of "Campanologists R Us". So they really had made a CD. He thought Kate had been joking.

Batt took a seat at the front of the lounge and explained that the first game was for a line. With participants, staff and visitors ready, he drew the first ball out of the barrel. He tried to ignore Hilda who was parading round the room showing everyone her hair-do.

'Legs eleven, number eleven.'

'Bingo!' said a voice.

'No Jean,' he said, 'you have to have a whole line of numbers. Next out is three and five, thirty five.'

'Bingo!' shouted the same voice, a little louder this time.

A member of staff moved to sit next to her. Hilda, pausing in front of the large mirror over the fireplace, declared Jean to be an idiot.

Batt thought it was going to be a long afternoon, and so it proved.

The session concluded with a squabble over who got which prize and was only settled when the retired headmistress bawled a few out and threatened to send them to stand outside her office.

He got a sympathetic smile from Sheila James as he packed the things away and left to seek refuge over a cup of tea in the kitchen. He made a mental note to find time to chat with her.

Chapter 11

The next morning he was in the middle of breakfast when his phone rang. He got up from the kitchen table and went over to where he'd left it on the work-surface. He was pleased to see it was Siobhan.

'Belfry,' said Batt.

'Very funny. You're up then, I take it. How's the back?'

'Still sore but it's easing up. I used some of that lotion you gave me. What was it, by the way?'

'Embalming fluid.'

He hoped it was her turn to be joking. Now that he thought about it, though, it did have a peculiar smell.

'So why the early-morning call?'

'Stoke haven't finished the autopsy on Tommy McCole but they have just confirmed his cause of death was almost certainly a massive intracranial brain hemorrhage. The bloods show nothing in the way of foreign substances such as sodium pentothal. At the moment they say they are not treating the death as suspicious. They're continuing with the autopsy this morning but given Tommy's vascular dementia they say it's what they would expect to find, especially when coupled with his diabetes.

Batt was surprised and disappointed. He had been certain there would be traces of the truth drug. It would have linked Tommy's and Kieran Wells's deaths. Now he would have to reappraise. The fact still remained that he had narrowly missed being run over and killed on the night of Tommy's death, but his belief that the driver had been Tommy's "cousin" was actually only an assumption. He hadn't been able to see who had been at the wheel. On the other hand if it was true Wells's killer had been trying to find the second British agent who had infiltrated the

IRA then McCole was probably the person most likely to hold the key – whether he knew it or not.

He was aware of Siobhan's voice on the other end of the phone.

'George, are you still there?'

'Sorry, Siobhan. It wasn't the result I was expecting. It's given my assumptions a knock. I'll have to rethink. But thanks for pulling a few strings.'

'My pleasure, but now you owe me.'

'OK. So what about a day out in north Derbyshire? We could visit Bakewell . There's lots of trendy shops you'd enjoy looking round and if you're lucky I might treat you to a Bakewell tart.'

'I think you mean a Bakewell pudding. A Bakewell tart is something completely different, and probably of greater interest to you than to me. By the way, Bakewell wouldn't happen to be anywhere near Monyash would it?'

Batt knew he had been rumbled.

'Well, as it happens… I could get a picnic together for the afternoon. For lunch I'll treat you to a slap up sandwich and a cup of tea at the Lambton Larder.'

'Hard to refuse. You don't give up easily do you?'

'Meaning what?'

"Meaning Tommy McCole.'

'So when are you free?'

'Monday suit you?'

Batt checked his wall calendar.

'I'm down for the nightshift on the Sunday but I could pick you up at about 11:00. It's only an hour's drive to Bakewell. We could start with lunch and then have a look round the town before a picnic in Monyash.'

'I'll look forward to it. If I hear anything of interest from Stoke I'll let you know.'

****

Monday saw Batt easing his car out of the parking place. Doing three consecutive night shifts at Mount View meant he hadn't had time to prepare a picnic, but he'd found an alternative. The forecast was for mainly dry weather with the chance of an odd shower. There was still warmth in the air even though it was overcast. He found himself looking forward to spending the day with Siobhan. She was easy company and good fun. She had been very supportive during Fran's illness, often volunteering to spend time with her so that Batt could disappear for a few hours to collect his thoughts.

She was waiting in the garden for him when he pulled up outside her cottage. She gave a smile and a wave and jumped in.

'Morning George. Work OK?'

'Pretty routine. The usual suspects getting up and walking the corridors, and Wilf treating the place like Colditz. Think I'll buy him a shovel for Christmas. He could then spend hours digging escape tunnels behind the workshops. Trouble is he'd probably succeed. How about we go the scenic route? Uttoxeter, Ashbourne, Alsop le Dale and Youlgreave.'

'Fine by me. Is this the way you and Fran used to come?'

'Yes. She liked Bakewell because of its connection with Jane Austen, and I loved mooching round the antique shops.'

'She loved her Jane Austen didn't she. I tried to persuade her to apply for 'Mastermind' but you know what she was like. What's Bakewell's connection to Jane Austen?'

Batt paused for a moment whilst he pulled out of the Five Lanes End junction near Draycot.

'Not keen on that bit of road. No-one seems to know who's got priority. Usually everyone sits there waiting for one another and when no-one moves everyone decides to go at the same time. It happened once when I was a passenger with Baz James on our way back from a training conference. Baz was used to this junction. I think he lived nearby at the time. Anyway, just before we got here he did what they do in American cop dramas – reached into the back seat for his magnetic bee-bah, wound his window down, stuck it on the roof and hit the play button. Instant success. The waves parted and we barely slowed down. He reckoned it worked every time.'

There was a break in the traffic and he pulled out onto the main road.

'Anyway, Bakewell and Jane Austen. Fran discovered that the Lambton in "Pride and Prejudice" was probably modelled on the town. Austen rewrote part of the story whilst staying at The Rutland Arms Hotel, so I suppose it makes sense. Mr Darcy's "Pemberley" was based on nearby Chatsworth House, so we often had to do a pilgrimage there as well.'

When he looked across at Siobhan she was busy brushing her hair.

'Not had time this morning. You weren't the only one up all night you know. We had a bit of a rush on yesterday. Bodies everywhere. I think the hot weather must have something to do with it. We worry about the elderly in cold weather but it's the summertime when they're equally vulnerable. Sorry, back to Jane Austen. Did you ever catch Fran's enthusiasm?'

Batt joined the A50 for a short stretch before turning off and taking the road to Ashbourne. As he went past the open prison he waved.

'Never know if any of my acquaintances might be looking out.

Jane Austen? I'd always dismissed it as a bit trivial, which was unfair because I'd never really given it a chance. Then when Fran was in her final stages I started reading 'Pride and Prejudice' to her and realised there was a lot of humour and social observation in it. I'll go back to it when I feel ready.'

'So the Lambton Larder where you're going to wine and dine me is so named because of the connection?'

'Yes. And believe it or not the owner's name is Jane. It's one of the few places to have cashed in on the link though, which is nice. No "D'Arcy Diner" or "Bingley Buffet"! On the other hand there are several places which pay homage to the Bakewell Pudding. The "Original Bakewell Pudding" shop is supposed to be where the pudding was accidentally concocted, but who knows. If shop names are anything to go by it seems tourists are more interested in their stomachs than their intellect.'

They carried on chatting and before he knew it Batt had driven through Ashbourne and into the Peak District National Park with its stone walls and fields of sheep, and was soon approaching Bakewell.

Once they'd found somewhere to park they headed straight for the "Lambton Larder". Batt had reserved a table for lunch and had ordered one of their excellent hampers to take with them for their visit to Monyash.

Afterwards they strolled down narrow cobbled streets admiring the mellow-stone Georgian buildings which housed a range of independent shops, before heading for the open market and finally back to the "Larder" to collect their hamper.

By the time they reached Monyash it was mid afternoon and the sun had come out. They parked by the village green and stretched their legs with a walk around the village. Despite its small size the village was a popular tourist attraction. A noticeboard on the edge of the green explained that there was evidence of a Neolithic settlement and that the famous stone circle and henge, Arbor Low, was built around 2000BC. Because of the many ponds created by the farmers thanks to the strata of clay, the village had become an important watering point for drovers on the intersection of several trade routes, and later on an industrial centre for lead mining. Its abundance of limestone had given it the title of the White Peak.

'How about a quick visit to Arbor Low?' suggested Batt. 'We can come back here and by then we should be ready to tackle the hamper on a bench in the churchyard.'

'I'd like that. The purpose of these stone circles seem to have archaeologists mystified. Let's go and solve it for them. Can't be that difficult to figure out.'

'It's about a six mile round trip so we'll go part way in the car otherwise it will be getting late.'

They set off past the stone-built primary school. The children in their red uniforms were being led to the gate by a teacher, where parents and grandparents were chatting as they waited. They drove through the stunning scenery of Lathkill Dale and on to Upper Oldhams Farm, where they parked. The path to Arbor Low was well trodden and several groups of people, many with dogs, were already returning to their cars.

Batt paid the parking charge and they set off.

Arbor Low, according to the National Trust display board, consisted of an earthen bank and ditch, with approximately fifty white limestone slabs which had all fallen. In the middle of the circle was a central stone.

'Perhaps it originally had a turfed roof,' suggested Batt. 'Maybe they held meetings here.'

They sat for a while taking in the panoramic view of the fells before making a quick visit to the nearby Gib Hill burial ground.

By the time they arrived back at Monyash it was late afternoon. Batt lifted the hamper from the boot of the car and they made their way to St. Leonards Church. It was an attractive Grade II* Listed stone building with a tall spire that could be seen for miles around. As Batt had thought, it was fairly isolated, the churchyard given a degree of privacy by some ancient trees. A yew tree by the main door was, according to a sign at its base, thought to be over seven hundred years old.

He put the hamper down in the porch and they went inside. It was pleasantly cool as they wandered up and down the nave and the two chancels which flanked it. The cream coloured walls gave it a relaxing feel, and they sat down on a pew near the rear, both sat lost in their thoughts as people had perhaps done since there had been a place of worship there for almost seven-hundred years.

'Do you miss Fran?' Batt suddenly asked.

'I miss her more than I can say, George. We all miss her – all her many friends. She was a very special person and she helped so many of us through difficult times. What makes you ask?'

'I was chatting to a lady in Bishops Bromley churchyard the other day. She asked the same question and I had to admit I'd never really thought about it – you know, that it's not just me who's been finding it hard to come to terms with her death.'

'Why do you think so many of her friends have stayed in touch? Apart from your magnetic personality and charm of course. It's our way of maintaining that link with her.'

Batt looked straight ahead and tried to study the stained glass window beyond the alter.

'You used to see a lot of her whenever I was away on a tour. I always appreciated that. Always knew she wouldn't be lonely.'

'I did it because I enjoyed her company, not through any sense of duty. There was a lot of talking done and a lot of laughing. And a lot of home-made cake eating. It was Fran who got me into singing with a choir. She said it was uplifting to sing with others. Not sure the choir leader quite shared her opinion when he heard me, though. One thing I never asked her was how you two got together. I know you went to the same university.'

'I was studying at the Keele Languages Centre – Arabic and Literature. Fran was studying French with a view to eventually teaching in a school. We had seen each other about the Centre but I never thought she'd really noticed me. I was too in awe of her to find out.'

'So who approached who?'

'It happened just after we'd finished uni. You know her father was a Scottish Presbyterian minister? Well he was officiating at the marriage of a friend of mine, and Fran was acting as his chauffeur. He must have been the world's worst driver and she always worried whenever he decided to get behind the wheel. She came into the church and recognised me of course, and came and sat with me in the congregation. You have to understand that I thought she was way out of my league so I was surprised. She could have had her pick of any of the men at uni. and there were a fair number of good looking athletic types who would have given their right arms for the chance to be seen with her. Instead there she was, sitting next to a language geek in some church or other, sharing a hymn book with him. At the reception we sat together and I happened to ask what she had planned for the summer. She said she was planning to go as a volunteer at Loch Lomand National Park and did I fancy joining her.'

A shaft of sunlight lit up the nave as the door was opened and two youngsters from the village school burst in. The boy held back but the little girl with bunches approached them.

'Excuse me, Sir, but our team has to find an old chest that's here in the church.'

Batt glanced at Siobhan and grinned.

She leant over and whispered in his ear, 'George Batt. Don't you dare say what you're thinking. Not in front of the children.'

Batt looked down at the floor as Siobhan said to the girl, 'There's a really old chest just down there at the end of the nave. I think it's eight hundred years old. Is that the one you've got to find do you think?'

She smiled her thanks and beckoned to the boy.

'Miss says it's down here. Come on.'

The pair of them raced down to the far end of the church and were soon absorbed in reading the information that was displayed.

Batt and Siobhan continued their conversation.

'So you went?'

'I did, and we just hit it off. I stayed with the family over the summer and we had a great time until it was time to go our separate ways.'

'You joined the army didn't you? How did that come about?'

'My language professor had called me in to his study just before Finals. He said there was someone I ought to meet. Turned out to be an army intelligence officer who said they were looking for someone with an aptitude for languages to train for Afghanistan. I'd nothing else lined up so after thinking it over for a few days I decided to give it a go. Fran, as you know, had already made plans to go and work in Malawi at a school her father had helped to found. We lost touch with one another for a couple of years or so. I assumed she'd found someone else and had forgotten about me.'

There was a clattering of feet as the two children raced excitedly back up the aisle, the girl shouting 'Thanks Miss' as they passed.

Batt turned to watch the boy struggle to turn the latch on the heavy oak door and pull it open. He raced off down the path leaving his team mate to pull it to behind her.

'We ought to go and sample that hamper,' said Batt, 'before your friends the flies get too interested.'

They had a last look around the ancient church before emerging into the sunlight and finding a bench in the shade of one of the lime trees.

Siobhan unpacked the hamper and they sat eating the scones and jam and drinking the elderflower cordial.

'So how did you both make contact again?' asked Siobhan.

Batt finished his second scone and wiped his fingers on a napkin before replying.

'When she returned from Africa she happened to meet up with a mutual friend who told her I was in Afghan still. It was my first tour since my passing out and for security reasons I couldn't be contacted. Fran went to see my parents and asked if they would get me to get in touch when I was next on leave. We picked up from where we had left off and every leave after that was spent together until finally my tour ended and we could set up home together in army accommodation.'

'You were in the Paras weren't you?'

Batt laughed.

'Not exactly *in* the Paras, Siobhan. I was attached to 3 Para as an intelligence gatherer. I don't think I could have managed their entry standards, certainly not the test that involved charging up some mountain in the Brecon Beacons with a fully loaded bergen. In fact I doubt I could even have picked the bergen up.'

'How many tours did you end up doing?'

'Two. The first was in 2006 and the second in 2008. In 2006 I was based in Kandahar City. 'KAF' we called it. There were something like 14000 troops and civvies based there and it really was like a city with burger bars, markets, banks, cafes and shops. The Paras thought those of us based there were having an easy time compared to them, and they were right. Whilst those in KAF were sitting in air conditioned ice-cream parlours or enjoying the delights of the Green Bean all-night coffee shop, the Paras were sleeping out in the open air on roll mats in terrific heat and being mortared by the Taliban every few hours. The mission then was to engage with the Taliban at every opportunity and drive them out of the towns and villages.

Then, when I went back in 2008 things had changed. It was all 'hearts and minds'. It was recognised the Taliban could not be defeated with firepower alone and so we tried to win over the people by building infrastructure like generators, drainage systems, schools and clinics.

The Afghan National Army was given a more prominent role in operations because it was felt the people trusted them more than the NATO forces.

The Taliban also changed tactics. Rather than confront our forces they developed a hit-and-run strategy. They also started to use IEDs which they could trigger by mobile phone. Spotters were all over the place, watching our troops as they moved and calling in their positions. They set off over 3000 bombs and IEDs that year.

Our commander was Mark Carleton-Smith and he decided we had to tighten control to the north of Gereshk. He had about eight thousand of us under his command. 3 Para was given the task of taking on the Taliban in Qal-e-Gaz and it was my job to find out where the Taliban were hiding themselves and their weapons. It was next to impossible, of course because either the villagers were too frightened to tell us anything or else the very people we were trying to sweeten up with money and gifts were actually members of the Taliban. To us they looked like ordinary farmers working in the poppy fields.'

Siobhan stretched and looked into the hamper. Her eyes lit up.

'Ooh look. A couple of individual Bakewell puddings. Lovely.'

She offered one to Batt who seemed lost in his thoughts.

'So did you have much success, George?'

'Sometimes. And sometimes not. I remember being given some intel by one of the villagers who told me Taliban forces were hiding out in a compound. I radioed it in and the Paras set off in some force. They were able to get pretty close to the building without any incoming fire. The Taliban either had a tip off and already left, or else the place was booby trapped and they were waiting until the troops got closer before setting off the bomb.

The lads said afterwards they were scared stiff as they advanced. Eventually they were close enough to lob a grenade through the doorway and when it exploded they rushed forward. When the dust had settled they looked in and found a goat calmly munching away at some hay.

They never let me hear the end of that one. In fact, to my shame, it's become part of 3 Para's folklore.'

She laughed.

'Well you can't win them all. Anyway at least you're still remembered by the regiment.'

He got up and stretched.

'When you're ready, do you fancy a look round the churchyard before we set off home?'

Siobhan finished her drink and Batt put the things back into the hamper.

'You trained at Liverpool, didn't you?'

'I did my science degree there and then joined the Scientist Training Programme for another three years to get my Masters before five years on a Higher Specialist Training Programme to get my Doctorate. My specialist research area was, of course, flies.'

She handed him her cup.

He hesitated before asking, 'You never married?'

It was more a question than a statement.

'I was nearly thirty by the time I had finished my studies and by then all the best men had been snapped up. Anyway, who'd want someone who spent all day furtling around with dead people's innards and who came home smelling of preserving fluid? Actually, come to think of it, if someone did find me attractive because of that then I don't think I would have wanted to marry them!'

They were walking back to the car when Siobhan decided she needed the loo. They went back to the church thinking there might be one there but they were out of luck.

'Looks like it's an al fresco job behind the trees,' she laughed. 'You go on ahead George and I'll meet you back at the car.'

He had just opened the boot to load the hamper when he heard a startled scream.

He raced back in the direction of where he had last seen Siobhan heading and found her pointing to a small memorial stone lying on the ground in a secluded area set aside as a sort of garden of remembrance. He read the inscription.

'Well, well,' was all he managed to say.

Chapter 12

Batt had a restless night. The date of birth on McCole's grave matched the date of birth on the documents he had seen in the office at Mount View, and the date of death was about a month before he had taken up residency there. It was too much of a coincidence for a case of stolen identity. But if it wasn't Tommy's ashes interred there then what was it? He came to the conclusion there was only one way to find out.

The weather had finally broken when he set out on a morning run. The sky was grey and by the time he had got as far as the church a fine drizzle had started to fall. He stopped under the lychgate and took a waterproof jacket out of his bergen. He was just setting off again when O'Brien's phone rang.

'O'Brien here. We've found the car. It's been torched. Middle of nowhere near a place in the Peaks called The Roaches. By the time Fire and Rescue got to the scene there was nothing much left for forensics. Seems like Brendan Quinn could still be hanging around. I've got people in the area.'

'How did he leave the scene? Has he got someone working with him do you think?'

'Probably by motorbike. There were tyre marks in the area left by a small bike.'

There was a pause and O'Brien asked, 'What are you doing? You sound like an old steam train.'

'Running off a few calories round the lanes.'

He was about to tell O'Brien about the discovery at Monyash churchyard but instinct told him to wait until he had found whatever it was that was buried there. He wondered whether he was becoming rather possessive about Tommy McCole.

'There's no point in you continuing at Mount View now that McCole is no longer with us. The person you were doing agency work for has made a miraculous recovery so you won't be needed again. Anyway, I have a feeling you'll be returning to work before long. The Police Complaints Commission will find there is no case to answer.'

O'Brien ended the call and Batt soldiered on up Narrow Lane and out into the countryside.

He'd gone past the farm where he and Tommy had stopped for cake, and taken a right turn towards the reservoir. By now the rain was becoming a deluge and he thought about turning back.

A van's headlights swept round a bend in the lane and Batt stopped and moved closer to the hedgerow to let it past. Only it didn't drive past.

It drew up alongside and, as Batt was wiping the rain from his eyes, the driver's door opened and blocked his path. At the same time the rear door also opened to cut off his retreat. The next thing he knew was he was being bundled in through a sliding side door by an unseen pair of hands and into darkness. He tripped and fell onto the van's floor and no sooner had he picked himself up than the van shot forwards and unbalanced him again.

A light was switched on. A man in a balaclava was sat on the wheel-arch, a Luger in his hand, the barrel pointing at Batt's head.

'Just to make sure we're giving a lift to the right person, please tell me your name.'

The accent was clearly Irish but more the Republic than the North.

Batt considered his options. They would clearly have a pretty good idea about the appearance of the person they had been told to lift so he assumed it was simply a test of whether he was going to be cooperative. Showing a willingness to cooperate might save him from a beating.

'You know who I am. George Batt.'

'Thank you Mr Batt. There is someone who wants to have a wee chat with you. Unfortunately he can't come to you so you're going to him. Now it's going to be a long journey so I suggest you make yourself comfortable.'

He indicated an inflatable bed and a travel bag.

'There's a towel in the bag. I suggest you dry yourself off and then change into the clothes you'll find in there. There's also something to eat and drink – but make it last because we'll not be stopping at any motorway services.'

Batt shrugged. He hadn't exactly much choice.

'Now hand me your bergen. I assume you've got a phone in there somewhere.'

Batt did as he was instructed.

The man threw him a pair of handcuffs.

'One cuff on your wrist and the other through that lashing point on the floor.'

When he'd done so the gun continued to be aimed at Batt's head whilst the man's other hand checked the cuffs were tight enough around his wrist.

'Nothing silly and you'll be OK. Like I said, someone wants to have a few words. If you can satisfy him then you'll be back home by this evening.'

He banged three times on the van's bulkhead and within a few minutes they came to halt and his minder disappeared through the rear door. He heard the passenger door open and close, the driver set off again and then the cargo light went out, leaving Batt in darkness.

Some time later they came to a halt. Judging by the way the van was lurching it seemed they had left the main road and driven onto some rough ground. The side door opened and the cuffs were removed. Batt looked out. The rain had eased but there was still a wind strong enough to rock the van.

'Where are we?'

'Anglesey. I hope you've got your sea legs on because you're in for a rough crossing. Now, nothing silly. Just follow me.'

He was led through some trees and down a rough track to where a Garda police car was waiting. His change of clothes, he realised, made him look like a prison inmate – grey tracksuit bottoms and a green top. He was made to sit in the back alongside a man in police uniform, who cuffed the pair of them together. Not a word had been spoken.

The journey to the ferry port of Holyhead was a short one. Once at the town they drove down a shabby residential street and into the holding compound. The Irish Ferries ship "Ulysses" was already docked and loading had begun. In different circumstances Batt might have enjoyed the view of the harbour with its backdrop of hills and modern suspension bridge which straddled it.

They waited in silence.

The ferry was enormous and seemed to dwarf the squat buildings. He studied its sleek shape. The red funnel bore the emblem of a shamrock, whilst the white sides of the hull bore the blue lettering of the shipping company. The modern image was enhanced by a swash of blue and green detailing, reminding Batt of similar styling he had seen on the sides of caravans.

Eventually, when all other vehicles had been loaded, the police car drove forward and up the ramp onto the ferry. There had been no need to show passports or any ID. They seemed to have been expected.

Batt, still handcuffed to his minder, was pulled out of the car and led up some steps to the passenger decks. He saw signs for the restaurant, bars, children's play area and cinema before climbing more stairs to where the cabins were. He got some strange looks from passengers as he was led down the corridor and was relieved when he was eventually pulled out of view and into one of the berths. The door was locked behind him and the cuffs removed.

He was spoken to for the first time since being handed over to the Garda.

'Toilet and shower over there. We'll be on board for about two and a half hours after which you've got a car journey of about the same length. Make yourself at home. There's a menu on the table. Let me know what you fancy. We'll be eating in here. As you've already been told, as long as you don't try anything on you'll be OK. And just in case you're feeling heroic there's an armed policeman outside the door.'

'Are you really the Garda?' asked Batt.

His question was answered by an icy stare.

The ship's engine started up and a tannoy announced that arrival in Dublin might be a little late because of the strong headwinds. The dock slipped by the cabin window and soon they were in open water.

It was mid afternoon when the ferry berthed at Dublin. Batt was handcuffed again and led back down the steps to the cargo deck and the car. Being last on meant they were first off. After the huge ramp had lowered they drove out of the terminal, were waved through security, and headed down O'Connell Street making for the M1.

Batt looked out at the wide pavements full of shoppers and tourists. There were some very grand buildings, none more so than the General Post Office and the Gresham Hotel. The stopped momentarily to allow a tram to trundle across in front of them. The statue of Daniel O'Connell stared back at him.

From the bustling O'Connell Street with its pavement cafes and bars they joined Parnell Street before heading through the suburbs on the M50 ring-road, leaving the city behind.

Once clear of any airport traffic, they made good progress. The motorway was remarkably quiet and they rarely had to drop speed from the seventy-five mph limit. Batt watched signs for Ballyriggan, Drogheda and Dundalk race by and soon they joined a stretch of dual carriageway which took them to the border close to Newry. It was here that they left the main road and headed for Flurrybridge before following signs for The Ring of Gullion. As they climbed, the views became even more breathtaking until they neared the highest point and looked down over the vast expanse of moorland and the lake. Their car pulled into a layby next to a sign for an ancient stone circle and before long they were joined by a Ford people carrier with blacked out rear windows.

Batt was pulled from the police car and into the rear of the other vehicle, his minder handcuffing him to a seatbelt anchorage point before throwing in his bergen and slamming the door shut.

'Welcome to the North,' was all that was said as they retraced their steps back to the M1 just north of Newry before crossing the border onto the N1.

Batt took stock of his situation. He was sharing the rear with an impressively large man who was wearing a black balaclava. In the hand furthest away from Batt was a pistol. The front seats were occupied by a man and a woman. The woman was driving.

It was late afternoon when they reached the outskirts of Belfast. Batt's world went dark as a hood was placed over his head.

When they eventually came to a halt his arms were cuffed behind his back and he felt a strong hand grabbing the back of his neck and pushing him forwards across some rough ground. He heard a metal door being opened and he was pushed inside. There was an empty-sounding echo as it was closed behind him. He was dragged across the floor and made to sit on a chair. Rope was wound around his chest and legs. Footsteps receded, the door opened and clanged shut, and he was left in the unsettling silence.

He recognised it as a typical ploy to play on his feeling of vulnerability. He'd seen it used often enough by the Paras. Those being interrogated were almost grateful when they were finally in the company of other human beings. He decided to use the time to think things through.

If he was in the hands of the Real IRA then it spelt trouble. As O'Brien had said, they were not interested in a political solution to the Northern Ireland problem. If they could reignite the violence by carrying out a few revenge killings then the situation would quickly get out of hand again. Batt knew he would be killed when it became clear he was of no use to them.

On the other hand, if he was dealing with the IRA then it was in their interest to nip any escallation of violence in the bud. They were in a strong political situation and at some point the Catholic majority would hold the balance of power.

Which of these two organisations had brought him here would become clear by the way they felt about the deaths of Kieran Wells and Tommy McCole.

He would soon find out. Footsteps approached him from behind and his hood was removed. He was in what was probably a disused warehouse – one of those with aluminium panels bolted to a steel frame. The concrete floor had at some time been marked out for shelving units and passageways for forklifts. The only natural light came from skylights in the roof. In front of him had been arranged a trestle table and chairs.

Through a door to his left came three men, all wearing black balaclavas. They seated themselves and the one in the centre addressed him.

'This is it,' thought Batt. 'IRA or Real IRA?'

'DI Batt. I'm sorry to have spoilt whatever you had planned today. If you co-operate then I promise you will be safely back in Bishops Bromley sometime later today.'

'And if I don't?'

'Then you won't be safely back in Bishops Bromley sometime later today - or anytime come to that. But let's not start out on the wrong foot. You and I may have the same objectives.'

'And what would they be?'

Batt's question was ignored. He had been trying to remember where he had heard that voice before. It was vaguely familiar.

'I was contacted by an MI5 officer asking if I could shed any light on the killing of a man named Kieran Wells. Apparently you were the Crime Scene Manager who read the pathologist's report and concluded that the presence of sodium pantothal together with an unusual piece of shrapnel probably linked the dead man to the Troubles. Would I be right in thinking this?'

'Yes,' said Batt. 'Together with a few other clues.'

'Both ourselves and your Intelligence forces were concerned that the death might have been the start of a mass settling of old scores. MI5's assumption is it's either an ex-paramilitary person or a current one. On the other hand who's to say it's not a former RUC officer or even an ex- member of the Paras. Let's face it, we none of us are getting any younger and if scores are to be settled then now's the time, before we go the way of all flesh.'

Batt suddenly knew the identity of the man behind the balaclava, and why that man had had Batt brought all the way to Belfast rather than interrogating him back on the mainland. He was a leading political figure whose travels would be monitored not only by the security forces but also the Press.

So, IRA not Real IRA. Batt gave a sigh of relief.

'I wasn't in a position to help MI5 but I knew someone who might.'

'Tommy McCole?'

'Correct. Because of his role with us, Tommy knew everyone. He had an almost photographic memory for faces. To many he was not only a valued member of our organisation but he was also a dear friend.

Now, a wee time after you were put in touch with him he ends up dead. Explain, if you will.'

Batt shifted his weight on his chair as best he could. His back was beginning to ache.

'Did Tommy have a cousin named Brendan Quinn?'

His interrogator looked in turn at the two men sitting either side of him. They both shrugged their shoulders.

'Being a good Catholic, Tommy had a fair few cousins but I'm not aware of a Brendan Quinn. Why?'

'He was visited in the care home on a couple of occasions by someone claiming to be his cousin. On the first occasion Tommy wasn't there but he was shown Tommy's room by one of the staff. The second occasion was the night Tommy died.'

'You're suggesting he was killed, which is exactly the conclusion we have come to.'

'Not necessarily killed,' said Batt. 'At least not directly by Quinn. Tommy died from a massive bleed to the brain. Whether it was brought on by whatever his visitor wanted, who's to say.'

'And what was it you think he wanted?'

Batt took a moment to consider before replying.

'Maybe not a possession. Most likely information Tommy held in his head – or should I say information Tommy might once have held in his head before his dementia took a hold. Probably a name.'

'Go on please Mr Batt.'

"I'm thinking this Brendan Quinn was almost certainly Kieran Wells's killer. He wanted him dead but first he wanted information – probably the whereabouts of someone else on his hit list - hence the use of sodium pentothal. Unfortunately the stuff was old and had increased in potency as a result. Quinn overdid it and Wells died before he gave anything away.

Who else might know what Quinn wanted to find out? Tommy McCole. If Quinn had the means to find Wells then finding Tommy's whereabouts would have been easy.'

'The name "Brendan Quinn" isn't familiar to us, but then it wouldn't be as it's unlikely to be his real name. We need to find him, Mr Batt. Any ideas?'

Batt made the decision to lay his cards on the table and give these three men what they needed. He hoped it would turn out to be the right call.

'I need my phone.'

'And why is that?'

'There's something on there that may help you.'

He watched as one of the men got up and went into what he assumed had once been an office or maybe a canteen. He returned with Batt's bergen. The one in charge unzipped it and pulled out both phones.

'Two phones?'

'One is my works phone. The other is for personal use. Turn on the one in the black case.'

He gave his password and saw the screen light up.

'Tap on "pictures". Scroll down and you'll come to one of a man in his fifties, thin-faced, earring in his left ear. That's who you're looking for.'

The three men stared at the image.

'Do you know him?' asked Batt.

'We're not sure,' the man in the centre said slowly. 'There is something about him that looks familiar but it's no more than that. Do you mind if we copy the picture?'

'Am I in a position to say no?'

The man laughed.

'I'll get one of our techs to use AI algorithms to give us an idea of what he might have looked like when he was younger. Thank you, Mr Batt. You've been helpful.'

'One more thing. He is probably still knocking around in the Bakewell area of Derbyshire.'

He went on to explain about the burnt-out car and the motorbike tracks.

It was one of the other two men who spoke for the first time.

'Which suggests whoever he is has unfinished business in the area. He doesn't know the whereabouts of the person he's looking for otherwise he wouldn't have needed to track down Tommy. If he learnt something from his visit to Mount View then he's hanging around in north Derbyshire because there's something there that will help him find whoever it is he's looking for. Either that or there's still someone else in the area he thinks holds vital information.'

'Me,' said Batt.

'Exactly. And do you have that vital information, Mr Batt?'

'Not that I'm aware of.'

The man had a whispered conversation with the other two before turning once more to Batt.

'So what do you intend doing now?'

'My investigation will concentrate on finding this so-called cousin and, if I can get enough evidence, charging him with the murder of Kieran Wells and attempted murder of Tommy McCole.'

'Do you have sufficient evidence, do you think?'

'Not enough for the CPS to press charges. It's nearly all circumstantial.'

'But you're pretty sure in your own mind that this Brendan Quinn is your man?'

'I don't think there can be much doubt.'

The main man took up the questioning again.

'Have you heard of the Green Book, Mr Batt?'

'The IRA's training manual.'

'Not just that. It also spells out the consequences should any member break the rules. I believe anyone falling foul of the code of conduct is given a fair trial – before they are either kneecapped or disposed of by the Nutting Squad. Do you understand what I am saying?'

'I think I've got your drift.'

'If he was one of ours we'll find him. If he was RUC we'll find him. If he's an ex Para…'

'Not ex Para,' interrupted Batt. 'Not with that accent.'

'You may be right. Whatever his background he needs to be stopped now, before others decide to follow suit and we end up with a mass of tit-for-tat killings that would almost certainly lead to Stormont being suspended again. We're very close to regaining what is rightfully ours, Mr Batt, something we've not had since the days of Cromwell. I'll not let anything derail us.'

The meeting seemed to have come to an end. The three men stood and left through the door by which they had entered.

One of the men who had been in the car that had brought Batt to the meeting appeared with his phone and bergen. He removed the restraints and handed back his things. Another man, pistol in hand, waited by the door.

Batt got up slowly and massaged his back.

'Another change of clothes for you. We don't want you arrested on suspicion of being an escaped prisoner. Here, put them on.'

Batt did as instructed.

'You will be returning to England by plane. You will be taken to Belfast City airport. You will find a ticket for a Ryan Air flight which leaves at 21:10. A taxi will be waiting at East Midlands to take you home. Your hood goes back on until we have left the city.'

His wrists were cuffed and he was led out to the car.

****

He arrived home just before midnight. He didn't know what was more exhausting – his day's ordeal or having to engage in discussions ranging from the fortunes of Burton Albion to the state of the economy with the taxi driver. What he did know was he was ready for a good night's sleep.

He walked round to the back of his house and made his way down the path. He unzipped a side pocket of his bergen and felt for his key. As soon as he unlocked the kitchen door he knew he'd had visitors. He'd been half expecting it.

Whoever had been in had been pretty careful not to disturb things, but not careful enough. Fran's photograph was at the wrong angle. The door to the living room had been closed. He shrugged. There was nothing he could do about it.

He fished his wet jacket out of his bergen and hung it up over the door to dry. He put his own phone on charge and O'Brien's on the kitchen table before switching off the light and going upstairs to bed. He was asleep almost immediately.

In the early hours of the morning he felt a hand grip his neck. He woke and had a strange sensation that someone was staring down at him. He'd had the nightmare before, but not recently. He'd been told it was PTSD, something a good many front-line military personnel suffered from. He thought he'd seen the back of it.

But then the hand gripped his neck again and Batt froze. He opened his eyes to see the dark eyes and sunken cheeks of a cadaver captured in the light shed by the street lamp outside the window.

Quinn.

Batt lunged at the face but the man stepped back out of range.

'Get up. Get dressed. We're going for a drive.'

Batt stared up at him.

'I've found the message Tommy McCole left for you. Careless of me not to have spotted it in his room, but careless of you to have left it in such a poor hiding place. Now get some clothes on and let's make a move. We'll be going in your car. The gun is loaded, by the way.'

He looked at the weapon. It was a Webley Mk IV, the same make as the one used to kill Kieran Wells. Batt had come across them in Afghanistan and knew cartridges were still manufactured in India even though the gun itself had not been manufactured since being retired from active service by the British military by the late 1990s. He seemed to remember it had been the weapon of choice for the Royal Irish Constabulary in the 1970s. He also seemed to remember it was deadly.

They made their way downstairs and Batt collected his keys from the drawer of the kitchen table.

'Do you know the way to Youlgreave,' he asked. 'If you don't then I'll need my phone.'

Quinn raised an eyebrow.

'For the sat nav,' he explained. 'Unless you want me to read a map in the dark whilst I'm driving.'

He picked up O'Brien's phone and put it in his pocket before Quinn had a chance to argue.

'I'll also need my credit card. I'm low on fuel.'

'I've got cash. Cards leave footprints.'

'Suit yourself but at this time of night the only way to get petrol is by using a card at a twenty-four hour service station.'

'Get it, then.'

'How about a torch? Graveyards are dark places.'

'Just get in the car, Detective Inspector.'

He followed Batt up the path, keeping a safe distance.

'Leave the key fob by the gate.'

He did as instructed and Quinn picked it up and pressed the button to unlock the car.

'Get in.'

Batt opened the car door and sat himself behind the wheel. He waited for Quinn to get in the back. Until the key fob was in the vehicle he couldn't start the engine. Quinn clearly wasn't stupid.

They set off, Quinn sitting directly behind Batt so it was impossible to see him through the rear view mirror.

Chapter 13

The roads were quiet, with just the occasional HGV or taxi passing in the opposite direction. They stopped for fuel at Ashbourne, pulling in to a brightly lit Texaco forecourt. Batt was aware that Quinn had lowered his window and had the gun trained on him whilst he operated the pump. Not that he was planning to escape just yet. There were things he needed to find out first.

He replaced the nozzle, retrieved his bank card and got back in the car. He hoped O'Brien's team were tracking him through the phone. He had assumed it was the reason for O'Brien's insistence he always had the phone with him. At this time of night, if his assumption was correct, it should have flagged up an alert at Hereford for unusual activity. If not it didn't much change things. He had a plan in mind and would keep to it.

He glanced at the phone's screen.

'We're about thirty minutes away,' he said as a means of starting a conversation. 'What do we do when we arrive?'

'We take a look around,' came the reply from the darkness behind him. 'McCole gave you instructions so it's in your interest to follow them.'

'What if we need to get into the church. The church will be locked. Did you think of that before dragging me out of bed in the middle of the night?'

'I doubt McCole will have left anything in the building. If he has then we wait until it's unlocked. I think it more likely he's buried something in some remote corner of the churchyard. Anyway, you've got the intel. Did he leave something in the church?'

Batt decided to change the subject. Telling Quinn where to look would, in Quinn's eyes, make him disposable.

'It was you who tried to run me over the night Tommy died. Why?'

'I assumed you were sent to get me. I didn't know at the time that you were going to lead me to whatever information McCole had hidden.'

'Did you know Tommy personally?'

Quinn must have decided that it didn't matter what Batt learnt about him. He wasn't going to let him live long enough to tell anyone.

'No. It was Da who worked with him. They were at the top table with the likes of James Drumm, Martin McGuinness, Sean MacStiofain, Seamus Twomey and Gerry Adams. Those five were Army Council. Tommy and my Da led the Security Council. It must have been the early '70s when Tommy McCole left to look after operations in England and at about the same time Seamus was arrested and ended up in Mountjoy - before the 'Provie Bird' landed in the exercise yard and rescued him. A daring escape which was hushed up by the Brits.'

'What was the Provie Bird? I've never heard of it.'

'Aye well you wouldn't. It happened in October 1973. The IRA borrowed a chopper and forced the pilot to land in Mountjoy's exercise yard. The prisoners made it impossible for the warders to get near it and by all accounts they didn't have to try too hard. It took off again with Seamus, J B O'Hagan and Kevin Mallon on board. Seamus was, as you know, Chief of Staff and O'Hagan was one of our key men. Mallon was someone you didn't mess with. He had been brutalised by his treatment at the hands of you lot. It was quite something.'

Batt brought him back to the Security Council.

'So who took the place of your da and Twomey?'

'Two so-called golden boys - Packie McWilliams and Andrew Kennedy. Seamus managed to stay on the run until late '77 when he and another Seamus, Seamus McCallum, were shopped. It was the last in a series of arrests of our top men which started with the arrival of McWilliams and Kennedy and ended when those two mysteriously disappeared just as the Nutting Squad were getting ready to put them on trial.'

He needed to keep Quinn talking. It wouldn't be long before they reached the place Batt had decided would be his point of no return. He gently pressed the button in the armrest that locked the windows, and also switched of the car's ABS.

'So presumably your father was part of this, him being on the Security Council?'

'It was Da who put two and two together and who compiled the evidence. They had got away with it for so long because Twomey and Adams made them untouchable.'

'Why so?'

'They had met Twomey in his local and got chatting. They seemed keen to join us. Twomey liked them and word is they met up several times during one summer. Said they owned an agricultural supplies business and could get hold of fertilizer for us. Twomey passed their names to MacStiofain who had them checked out. Their business seemed legit. With supplies from America constantly being intercepted we couldn't believe our luck. Mac did the usual and put them to the test.

They were tasked with mortaring an army patrol just south of Armagh along the so-called 'murder mile'. The plan was to drive to a local park and leave the van set up ready for later. Somehow the army were tipped off.

When McWilliams and Kennedy returned later that evening they were met by a missile fired from a rocket launcher. They were both injured, McWilliams quite badly so I'm told. Despite this they managed to set off one mortar before they disappeared from the scene. MacStiofain was impressed and they quickly rose through the ranks. It seems they could do no wrong.'

'McWilliams and Kennedy got wind of the checks your da was doing on them?'

'Obviously. They vanished, so they did, back into the grateful arms of the Brits.'

'What aroused your da's suspicions about them?'

'Until their appointment on the Security Council the IRA had been enjoying some success against the army and the RUC. Then our luck seemed to run out. There were minor successes, of course, but it was mainly against property rather than personnel. When it came to using IEDs against army personnel they as often as not failed to detonate. We also experienced a rise in the numbers being picked up and put in internment.

Perhaps that's where you Brits made a big mistake. Suspected IRA men were housed in separate wings from other prisoners and allowed to mix freely with each other. They swopped stories about their arrests and made sure Da got to know what their thoughts were. Their theory was that someone was dampening the fertilizer so it wouldn't detonate.

McCole was suspected at first. He had always made it known he thought the killing of Irish civilians was counter-productive. He wanted our bombing campaign to be directed at political high-ups on the mainland. He reckoned if they feared they would be targeted then they were more likely to be cooperative. Anyway, when McCole moved to England and many of the bombs still failed to go off we knew it wasn't him. McWilliams and Kennedy were then the obvious ones to investigate – and they knew.'

Batt reckoned they were no more than six minutes away from his chosen spot, but there was one thing he needed to find out first.

He very gently gathered speed whilst asking about the murder of Kieran Wells.

'Wells. Aka Packie McWilliams, you mean. His name and identity were changed to Kieran Wells by army intelligence and for a while he was given round-the-clock protection. But I knew I'd catch up with him sooner or later, just as he knew I would. Just as the other one, Andrew Kennedy, knows.'

The car drew onto the straight piece of road that Batt had been waiting for. The speed had crept up to nearly seventy. Quinn was unaware.

'What I don't understand is why you want them dead.'

The reply came as an angry shout.

'Because on the night they were pulled they killed my da and took the evidence. Shot him in cold blood in the street as he was coming home with my birthday present. How could…..'

Batt stamped on the brakes and braced himself against the steering wheel. The car slewed wildly, throwing Quinn towards the other side. At the same time, Batt had opened his door and rolled out onto the road. He was up and running before Quinn had had time to undo his seat belt.

Realising he couldn't lower the window to take a shot at the disappearing figure, he kicked open the rear door and took off after him.

Batt raced across the lay-by, hurdled a fence and made for the line of trees, zig-zagging as he went. He was half way there when he heard the pop pop of the gun. He knew from experience that if you could hear the gun then the bullet had missed its target. He ploughed on, finally crashing through bracken and thorn bushes before disappearing into the blackness of the woods.

Which way? He desperately tried to remember which direction would give him the most cover. He reckoned on south because further up the road, to the north, was a disused aerodrome which had been taken over by a motorcycle club. Darley Moor Motorcycle Racing. He and Fran had been caught up in the meet traffic on more than one occasion as they made their way to Bakewell, Chatsworth House or Haddon Hall. The Jane Austen trail. All this was going through his head as he battled through the undergrowth. He hadn't gone far when he made out what looked to be a path. Maybe a footpath, maybe a path made by the deer. He decided to take it in the hope of putting some distance between himself and Quinn.

A hundred or so yards later he stopped for a moment and listened. Quinn hadn't looked particularly fit, in fact he looked ill, but he could be heard not too far behind. He was making enough noise to mask any that Batt made and so he decided to run on until he came across somewhere suitable for an ambush. No point in hiding because Quinn would keep searching until he had found him.

The opportunity came a few minutes later. He could just make out a small clearing with a cluster of bushes in the middle.

He removed his jacket as he ran and draped it over the end bush before making his way into the cover of the trees again and circling back to a place on the path where Quinn was likely to first see it. The army called it the 'distraction technique'. The brain would take a second or two to interpret the information the eyes fed it. In that moment's hesitation you struck.

He desperately felt around for a stout piece of wood to use as a weapon. Quinn could be heard not far away, breathing heavily. Batt gave up the search and hid himself in the undergrowth, feeling for something solid that would give him purchase when he sprang for Quinn's legs.

He controlled his breathing and waited.

The footsteps came closer and closer to where he was hiding and stopped just ahead of him. He peered through the bracken and saw Quinn doubled up with his hands on his knees peering at the dark outline of the jacket and bush.

In that moment Batt sprang, aiming for Quinn's knees. He hit him with some force and the pair of them hit the ground knocking the wind out of Batt's lungs. The other man rolled away and scrabbled around in the dark trying to find the gun that had been sent flying. Batt tried to get to his feet but Quinn's kick found the side of his head and floored him. He staggered up just in time to see the gun being pointed at his head. Quinn's finger tensed on the trigger as he took up the pressure. Batt looked him in the eye.

'You kill me and McCole's secret goes with me.'

Quinn backed away and leant against a tree, trying to get his breath back.

'Inconvenient but all it does is delay things. Youlgreave churchyard can't be that big. It's taken me years to get this far. Another day or two won't matter.'

Batt reached up and felt the side of his face. He felt the stickiness of blood. He wiped his hand on his trousers.

'But time is a luxury you haven't got. Am I right? You're on borrowed time by the looks of you.'

'You might be correct in that observation, Batt, but it's longer than the time you've got left.'

'And what if I were to tell you you'd be looking in the wrong place? That the information you desperately want that you hope will lead you to Kennedy is not at Youlgreave?'

He saw Quinn's body tense and a look of doubt cloud his face.

'You forget that I found McCole's message that you'd hidden in that clock.'

'Not McCole's message. My message. Do you think I'm stupid enough to leave it in such an easy place for someone like you to find ?'

'You're lying!' yelled Quinn.

'But if I'm not, and you shoot me, you can say goodbye to any thoughts of revenge on Kennedy.'

He could see the man begin to waver before making up his mind and raising the gun again.

'I'll take my chance. Anyway you were a dead man walking the moment you got in the car.'

He took aim and Batt backed away down the path before tripping and ending up on his back. He looked up to see the barrel pointing down at him.

There was a loud crack and Batt felt blood running down his chest and arms. Then Quinn dropped like a stone.

An Irish voice called out from the darkness of the trees to his left.

'Batt. Don't move. Stay where you are.'

A figure dressed in black wearing a balaclava emerged. He pulled a pistol from his belt, stood over Quinn and fired a shot into his head.

'Can't be too careful, Come on then, up you get. You can't stay there all night.'

He reached down and held out his hand.

'Sorry about the state of your clothes. You'll need to get changed.'

He removed his backpack and reached into it.

'Recognise these?'

Grey jogging bottoms and a green top.

'And here's something to stick over that cut on your head. Be quick.'

He handed over a large plaster that he took from a field dressing first aid pack.

Another figure emerged from the trees behind Batt. He was pulling an earpiece out from under his hood with one hand whilst the other carried an Armalite M16. Under his arm was Batt's jacket. He studied Quinn's body for a moment before telling his colleague that the Cleaners were on their way. He reached down and searched through the pockets until he found Batt's car keys.

Whilst getting out of his bloodied things Batt asked the obvious question: 'So how did you know I was in trouble?'

He had the feeling the man was smiling behind his balaclava.

'After we picked you up yesterday morning, a man was sent to search your house.

When he arrived he found he'd been beaten to it. Someone else was already giving the place a going over. We told him to simply observe but not to get hands-on. By the time your friendly taxi driver got you home last night this visitor was still inside. We texted our man the picture you gave us of Quinn that you had on your phone. He reckoned it was probably a match.'

Batt handed over his clothes which were put into a plastic bag and they started to walk back the way they had come.

'Anyways, we reckoned you were worth more dead than alive to Quinn and so we waited. Sure enough the two of you emerged in the wee small hours and drove off.'

'But I didn't see any headlights in my rear view mirror,' said Batt giving his face another dab.

'No need to follow you. We've had a tracker on your car for a good while – by now it will have been removed.

My friend here was nearly caught out by the two thugs who attacked you in your garden. He hung around to see if you needed any assistance but from what I gather you more than took care of them.'

Batt thought back to that night and to the figure he thought he'd seen disappearing up the lane.

'When it was obvious which way you were heading we had cars stationed along the route and sent up a drone to follow you from above. It did take us a bit by surprise when you made your emergency stop, mind you. The drone's thermal imaging camera soon picked you up but it still took us a few minutes to reach you in those woods. Fortunately we made it in time.'

They emerged from the woods and climbed over the fence. Batt could see his car parked in the lay-by, alongside a Transit van and a Volvo estate. Two other men were putting on rucksacks which they'd taken from the van and were disappearing into the darkness to retrieve Quinn.

'Here are your keys, Mr Batt, and your jacket. We'll follow you back to Bishops Bromley just to make sure you get home safely. Or if you're not feeling up to it one of us can drive your vehicle for you?'

Batt took the keys and walked towards his car, but stopped and turned towards the men.

'I've only ever known him as Quinn. Was that his real name?'

'When our technical team used the photograph you gave us to reverse-age him, he bore a strong resemblance to one of our top men from the 70s. He was murdered on his way home one night.'

Batt nodded.

'He was going to his son's birthday party. He had a present for him. Quinn told me in the car. Revenge is best served cold, as they say. I'm not going to be told who he was am I?'

'No, Detective Inspector.'

Batt held out his hand.

'I guess I should thank you.'

'No need, Detective Inspector. It's what we do. It isn't the first time and sadly I doubt it will be the last that we've had to look after our own. The end will justify the means, to quote another well known phrase. Drive safely.'

Batt arrived home just as the day was breaking. He parked up and stood for a moment looking at the sky. Red sky in the morning: shepherd's warning. Not that they needed it, he thought. Probably saw the forecast last night on the internet. Or got a warning on their mobiles.

He was very tempted to go back to bed but felt he ought to contact O'Brien first.

He made himself a coffee, took it into the lounge and pressed speed dial. Within a couple of rings it was answered.

'O'Brien.'

'Good morning Mr O'Brien. You're up early. Were you expecting me to ring?'

'For your information I'm not up early. I'm still in bed.'

'I'm glad one of us can get some sleep.'

'Who said anything about sleep? I hope this is worth it. Hang on whilst I make my way to the office.'

Batt heard a door close and then O'Brien spoke again.

'What's the news?"

Batt took a sip of his coffee, deliberately making O'Brien wait.

'You mean you don't know?'

'If you tell me what it is you've rung about then I'll tell you whether I know or not.'

Batt though he detected a slight air of impatience. He took another sip of coffee.

'You know I have spent the early hours of this morning looking down the barrel of Quinn's gun whilst taking him for a joy ride to Youlgreave.'

What O'Brien said next surprised him.

'How am I supposed to know that?'

'But weren't you monitoring me on the phone you gave me?'

'Monitoring you? What made you think that?'

'I assumed that's why you told me to have the phone with me at all times.'

'Mr Batt, do you really think we've the resources to keep tabs on you and others like you? We struggle to keep track on what the Russians and Chinese are up to – and they could start World War Three. You're surely not suggesting you're up there with the likes of them are you?'

'Do you mean to say I've never had any back-up? So why tell me not to go anywhere without the phone you gave me? '

'Just in case you had anything to report for us to act on. Look, the first time we met I thought I made it clear we are Intelligence. We pass information we think important to relevant organisations. We don't get our hands dirty.'

A sick feeling came over him. Since day one he had been acting alone. No back-up. He had always found reassurance from the belief that others were looking out for him. Just like his time in Afghanistan. No matter how much trouble you were in you knew your mates would risk their own lives to pull you out of it. He had been set up. He was a stalking horse, a pawn who could be sacrificed for something deemed more important than his own life. But what was it? What was it that meant his life could be weighed against that of the likes of Kieran Wells and judged to be less important? Kieran Wells was dead. Tommy McCole was dead.

Kennedy. It had to be Kennedy.

'Are you still there, George?' came O'Brien's nasal voice.

Batt measured his words carefully.

'Quinn had me at gunpoint. He was just about to kill me. What would have happened if the IRA's enforcers hadn't turned up?'

'Then you wouldn't be talking to me now. But they did turn up.'

'Acting on an intelligence tip-off?'

'I'll leave that to you to decide. Tell me, Detective Inspector, what did you learn about Quinn?'

Batt was tempted to end the call but he'd had enough of O'Brien and his deceptions and just wanted him gone.

'Quinn was acting on his own. He was out to get revenge on the two who murdered his father – Wells, or should I say McWilliams, and his partner Kennedy. Wells's death and Tommy McCole's death was nothing to do with any paramilitary group. I don't think this will be the start of renewed sectarian violence as a result of Quinn's actions.'

'Good. Then I must thank you and say goodbye. You can keep the phone but you'll need a new sim card. The one it came with will no longer work when I end this call.'

The line went dead, leaving Batt staring at the blank screen. He sat back in his chair and closed his eyes. There was something that didn't add up. Something that, in his own time in army intelligence, he would have been able to identify.

Outside the window traffic was beginning to build up as people set off for work. A lorry's air brakes hissed as it juddered to a halt waiting for the stream of oncoming vehicles to clear. Then the outside world became more distant, muffled, and he drifted off with the empty mug still in his hands.

****

He was woken sometime later by the sound of the postman pushing mail through the letterbox. He checked the time. Nearly eleven o'-clock. He had pins and needles in his left arm. He flapped it about until the feeling came back.

He got up and took his phone off charge. There was a missed call, he noticed. Whoever it was could wait. He went into the kitchen and opened the fridge door. There was nothing much on the shelves. He'd have to drive to Uttoxeter and get some things if he was going to have any dinner. Either that or book himself a table at one of the village pubs. He decided to combine a shopping expedition with a visit to Mount View to say his goodbyes.

He showered, put a fresh plaster over the cut on his face and collected his car keys. After a quick inspection of the car – new front tyres needed – he set off.

The town was quiet and it didn't take long to get what he needed. It was about mid day when he pulled up into his usual place in the care home's car park, next to a Skoda bearing Rumanian number plates. He smiled as he made his way to the main door and rang the bell. It was opened by Miriana who hugged him and then made a shushing sign with her finger. She led him towards the dining room. He could see the usual residents seated in their usual places, some chatting and others staring vacantly. Miriana pointed to a table at the far side of the room. Facing him were two men and with her back to him was Maria. They were laughing and chatting excitedly. Miriana made her way over to them and said something. Maria turned round and leapt to her feet. She rushed over and threw her arms around him before dragging a self-conscious Batt over to her table.

' George. I want you meet my family. This is husband Marku, and this is son Alin.'

The two men got to their feet and shook his hand. Both were surprisingly tall, in contrast to Maria.

Marku invited him to join them at the table and they soon got chatting. Alin was a little more reserved but polite. His English was excellent thanks, he said, to listening to English music and American tv shows. The majority of young Rumanians were similarly fluent.

Kate appeared in the doorway and came across.

'George. How lovely of you to call in. You will stay for dinner. It's cottage pie,' she added, knowing Batt wouldn't refuse. 'I'm so sorry you're having to leave us. We all are. May I ask for you next time we're short-staffed?'

Batt made the right noises, and felt sad it would never happen.

'I'm glad you're here. It's Tommy McCole's funeral tomorrow. I tried to let you know by phoning your agency but the line seemed dead. It will take place at Tixall Road Crematorium at two-thirty. I know you two got on well together. Will you be able to come?'

Batt nodded and she continued, 'I can't see that anyone other than us will be there. You didn't manage to find Tommy's cousin before he left for Ireland?'

'He must have moved out of the area before the police could track him down. Who are the undertakers?'

'We always use the Co-op in Uttoxeter when the deceased is someone like Tommy without any relatives that can be traced.'

She patted his shoulder and moved off, doing the rounds of the other tables. He watched her as she helped cut up dinners or gave encouragement to those who seemed lost. It took a special type of person to work in a residential home and she had assembled a good team.

During the course of the meal Batt learnt that Marku was planning to take Alin to Birmingham at the weekend for Freshers week, before starting the long journey back to Polietsi. This time would be a brief visit to England but he said he hoped to return later in the autumn to spend more time with Maria. They said their goodbyes but not before they had persuaded Batt to join them after Tommy's funeral for a traditional Rumanian meal back at the flat Maria rented. Sarmale and ciorba de burta were on the menu.

As he made his way out of the dining room he caught the eye of Hilda who winked and waved a stick at him. Sheila, who was sitting next to her, turned to see who she was goading and gave him a wave. Hilda and Sheila seemed unlikely bed-fellows. But not as unlikely as MI5 and the IRA.

Chapter 14

A good night's sleep had refreshed Batt. He had been up at a decent time and had managed a run around the lanes before breakfast. In contrast to the last few weeks, autumn didn't seem far away. A few trees were beginning to change colour and there was a thin mist which hung over the reservoir. As a boy it was at this time of year he and his friends had always gone scrumping down in Mellor's orchard. He suspected Mr Mellor had been aware because a ladder was often conveniently left at the side of the barn.

He remembered the missed call from yesterday and switched on his phone. Two more messages pinged through, all three from Pete Jones. The first read "Her ladyship requests the pleasure of your company at 09:30am tomorrow", the second "The Chief expects you in her office this morning at 09:30" and the third "Get yourself down to the Station NOW or she'll kill you."

The third message had been sent twenty minutes ago.

Batt returned the call and a relieved detective superintendent told him he had thirty-two minutes to save his bacon.

'What is it that's so urgent, Pete?'

'She's going to beg you to return to work. The Force is unable to function without you. Only you, Batt Man, can save the city.'

'Burton isn't a city, it's a town,' Batt pointed out.

'Just between you and me, George, you've been completely cleared by Police Complaints of any misconduct and no mention of the enquiry will appear in your records. In fact, from what I understand, the report recommends you should be congratulated on the work you have done in the community. Twenty-nine minutes. I take it it's mission accomplished?'

'I think you could say that. It's been an interesting experience but not one I'd want to go through again. I'll stick to petty crime in Burton. At least I feel more in control there. I better set off. What colour shoes is she wearing, by the way?'

'I think they're back to red. She had bright blue on yesterday for her radio interview.'

'For her what?'

"Twenty-seven minutes."

The call was ended.

Twenty-five minutes later and Batt was standing outside Ms. Foster-Goode's door, listening. He heard the end of Aretha Franklin's "RESPECT" followed by the intro music to Radio Burton's mid-morning show. Which wasn't on air until ten-thirty. Which meant, he deduced, she was listening to her interview of yesterday on BBC Sounds.

The red light was on but he knocked and entered. She looked up from her i-phone and hastily turned it off.

'You wanted to see me Ma'am. At nine-thirty. I appear to be a couple of minutes early. I can wait outside if you like.'

'Let's get this over with Batts. You have been cleared to return to work . I shall expect you to report for duty tomorrow morning.'

He noticed her looking at the cut on his face.

'Gardening leave can be a dangerous thing Ma'am.'

She looked down at some document on her desk, a sign that his audience was over.

Batt coughed and she peered over her glasses at him.

'Can I see a copy of the Commission's report? If there are any suggestions as to how I can improve the effectiveness of my people-management moving forwards then I would like the opportunity to take them on board. Ma'am.'

She gave him a withering look and Batt was sure he saw an eye twitch.

'Anything, Ma'am?' he persisted.

'No Detective Inspector. Nothing has been recommended. That will be all.'

'Yes Ma'am. Oh, will it be OK if I call in to see Blue Team before I leave?'

'Yes. You will find they have made good progress in your absence.'

It was Batt's turn to twitch.

Back out in the corridor he caught sight of DI Mills.

'DI Mills,' he shouted. 'How's the Kieran Wells murder case coming on?'

Mills did his best to pretend not to have heard but Batt caught him up.

'Any more arrests in the pipeline?'

'Ah, Batt Man. The grapevine says you're in the clear then? Runner beans been fighting back?' he asked, catching sight of the damaged face that was smiling a little too broadly at him.

'Arrests? Any nearer to solving the murder?'

'Our investigation is ongoing.'

'*Our investigation is ongoing*? Is that Foster-Goode speak for we-stand-as-much-chance-of-solving- this-as-finding-Lord-Lucan. And-Shergar?

Having-dinner-together,' he couldn't help adding.

'I'm expecting a breakthrough soon, OK?' said a clearly ruffled Mills as he sought refuge by disappearing into the gents.

Batt went back downstairs and opened the door to his team's office. Several heads turned in his direction and frowns turned to smiles. Helen jumped up and hugged him, much to Batt's embarrassment, whilst Chris and Baz shook his hand.

'Don't even think about asking how I got this,' said Batt pointing to his face. 'I did it shaving is the official line.'

'What on earth were you using? A machete?' asked Helen.

'We had a tip-off you would be back,' said Baz. 'Here, we got you a welcome home present, Sir.'

Chris produced a box of coffee pods.

'So do I take it you lot have used up the ones I left behind? You do know that using a DI's coffee machine in his absence is sackable offence? Did you get any biscuits to go with them, by any chance?'

Helen opened the stationery cupboard door to reveal three large tins of Elkse's deluxe chocolate selection.

'Thought we'd support local business, Sir.'

'Well let's have a brew and whilst we're waiting you can fill me in on how you've been getting on.'

The smiles flickered and then vanished.

'To be honest, Sir,' said Baz, 'we were just beginning to get on top of things when the Chief did another radio interview yesterday.'

'Don't tell me it was about hate crime?'

'Yes Sir. She was going on about her Twitter thingy named #ShowRespect. Helen's already a follower. Have you seen the foyer? It's full of people wanting to file complaints.'

'Right,' said Batt. 'Come with me. Not you Chris. You're going to make sure we've all got coffee and biscuits waiting for us when we get back. And in case you don't know, my favourite is the biscuit wrapped in silver foil.'

Baz and Helen hurried after Batt as he walked determinedly down the corridor to reception. Annette looked up from her keyboard, welcomed him back, and passed him a handwritten note. He read it and smiled. It was from Dean telling him the goal nets had arrived and thanking him. He put it in his pocket and walked over to where several members of the public were staring up at him from their blue plastic seats. He took his time studying each of them in turn.

'Right. If we have any cross-dressers who have come to file a complaint that someone on a supermarket checkout has called them 'Sir' then they can make for the exit now.'

He stood open-mouthed as someone stood up and left.

'I was joking,' he whispered to Helen.

'Now,' he continued, 'there has been a rumour going round that the police will pay compensation to anyone who has been on the receiving end of a hateful comment. I'm sorry to have to tell you that the rumour is false. If that's your reason for coming then there's the door.'

Four more disgruntled members of the public made their way out.

Batt counted five people remaining.

'Is anyone here for any reason not connected to hate crime?'

'Yes,' said a young woman. 'I'm afraid I've got a problem with my neighbours.'

' OK,' said Batt. 'Would you like to explain to the person on reception and we'll try to get you sorted?'

He turned to the remaining four.

'We'll be with you as soon as we can. I have three officers who will take some details from you, but please be patient.'

He beckoned to Baz and Helen to follow him back to their office.

'A quick coffee and then you'd better go and take some details from them. I'm not officially on duty until tomorrow so I'll disappear soon –anyway I've a funeral to go to in Stafford.'

'Oh I'm sorry Sir,' said Helen. 'Someone you were close to?'

'In a way,' said Batt. 'Although I'd only known him for a short while. See you all tomorrow.'

He made his way out past the waiting complainants, assuring them his officers were on their way.

He drove across the other side of town to an automotive centre and was told they had a couple of budget tyres in stock and the car would be ready in about an hour.

He set off walking to Halfords. The roads were, as usual, busy and their was a tailback all the way from the bridge over the Trent. He crossed over and decided to kill some time by walking through the wetlands. It was part of the river's flood plain and the council had developed it as a peaceful open space. It was clearly a hit with dog walkers and people pushing buggies. Batt kept to the path and entered a wooded area before crossing a footbridge and coming out to the rear of a row of retail units.

He pushed open the door of the motorist store and went through his mental shopping list. He walked up and down the aisles until he had found what he was looking for. Next stop was Dunelm, where he bought a pack of four knitting needles.

By the time he had walked back to the garage, his car was ready waiting for him. He dumped his shopping in the boot, paid the bill and drove home, stopping off at the Bishops Bromley village store for some flowers and a bottle of wine.

He grabbed a quick shower, got changed into the suit he had last worn at Fran's funeral and went downstairs for a bite to eat. Before leaving he phoned the undertaker's and arranged to have Tommy's ashes saved and then he set off for Stafford.

The crematorium was sited in the countryside with Cannock Chase in the distance. Batt turned off the main road and into the grounds.

The building itself was a modern single-storey affair approached from a long driveway lined with rose bushes and ornamental trees. It was surrounded on three sides by a car park that was too small to accommodate the volume of traffic the conveyor belt schedule of services required. Consequently cars were lining the driveway and people were making their way on foot.

He was half an hour early and so one lot of mourners were leaving and another lot arriving. He watched as a hearse left from a side exit as another waited a respectful five minutes before pulling up under the canopy at the main entrance. The immediate family got out to be greeted with hugs and sympathy from those already waiting. Two undertakers in top hats slid the coffin out and wheeled it round the corner of the building on a guerney. The mourners were ushered inside and the main doors were closed behind them.

Batt moved into a parking space vacated by a young family who had been attending the previous service, and sat and waited. In his jacket pocket he found a copy of the eulogy he'd been unable to deliver at Fran's funeral. The vicar had seen his distress and read it for him. He started to read through it but his vision blurred and he found himself feeling alone and crying.

He had just about recovered when the Mount View minibus drove slowly past and reversed into one of the disabled bays. He got out and walked over. Kate was at the wheel and she waved him over.

He helped everyone off and shepherded them towards the main doors where they sat and waited in silence, seemingly lost in their thoughts. A couple of the care staff had come with them.

Batt walked back to the minibus where Kate was locking up.

'George. Thank you for coming. I've a favour to ask.'

He looked at her questioningly.

'Can you sing "The Fields of Athenry" at the funeral? I'd do it myself but I can feel a sore throat coming on.'

She saw the look of terror on his face.

'I'm joking. Would you, though, read a poem? Or should I say the last bit of a poem? It's only a few lines by Robert Test. He was an American poet who campaigned for organ donations – not possible in Tommy's case I'm afraid but I thought the last few lines were appropriate. Will you?'

'I'd be honoured,' said Batt.

She handed him a copy and went over to stand with the others.

He looked at the text and agreed with Kate. It did seem appropriate.

A hearse had passed through the crematorium gates and was waiting halfway along the drive.

Very soon the side doors of the chapel opened and people began to drift out in twos and threes. At about the same time the main doors opened and the hearse moved forward. Those waiting were ushered into a foyer and held there for a few minutes before being allowed into the chapel. Peaceful cream walls and ceiling, a few neat rows of burgundy-coloured conference chairs, and an inappropriately positioned notice above a door at the front which read 'Fire Exit'.

Piped organ music played something nondescript whilst the small gathering seated themselves and then the same vicar who had braved the care home with his crimpolene choir appeared and stood before the lectern. He fiddled with the microphone and gave it a few taps to make sure it was working before saying a few words about the man he had never known. A CD played the opening bars of 'The

Lord is my Shepherd' and the vicar found himself singing almost solo, almost, that is, until a beautiful soprano voice joined him. Batt looked across and saw it was Hilda. The world was full of surprises.

When his turn came, he walked to the front and paused.

'I only knew Tommy for a brief time, but in that time I felt I had met a man who was finally at peace with himself and the world.'

He read from the piece of paper Kate had given him.

'Burn what is left of me and scatter the ashes to the winds to help the flowers grow.

If you must bury something, let it be my faults, my weakness and all prejudice against my fellow man.

Give my sins to the devil.

Give my soul to God.

If, by chance, you wish to remember me, do it with a kind deed or word to someone who needs you.'

After the service he drove to Uttoxeter and found the funeral parlour where he payed what he owed for Tommy's ashes before going back home to get changed into something more suitable for dinner with Maria and her family. He was looking forward to that part of the evening but not to what was to follow.

****

When he left her flat a few hours and a considerable number of calories later, it was beginning to turn foggy. At Ashbourne he filled up with petrol at the same garage he had used the night before and arrived in Monyash at about midnight.

The place was deserted. Only the odd light was still on in the cottages he passed before he entered the lane on the far side of the village green and pulled to a halt. He got out and lifted his bergen off the back seat and then stood for a moment to allow his eyes to adjust to the darkness. He breathed in the smell of the pine trees under which he'd parked. Somewhere in the distance a dog barked.

The church was across the green and down a lane.

He locked the car and set off, keeping an eye out for any sign of movement. The fog seemed to be thickening and the absence of any street lighting made it difficult for him to get his bearings. He passed the entrance to a farm and remembered it from the last time he was in the village. A dog had come running out barking at Siobhan and making her jump before it decided to call off the chase and saunter back towards the farm yard.

The lane leading to the church suddenly appeared on his left. He reckoned the entrance was about fifty metres down. He stood for a moment, listening for any human sounds, and satisfied he was not being followed, he walked on.

The approach to the church from the lane was down a gravelled driveway. Batt kept to the grass verge on the left until he arrived at the tarmac path that would take him to the rear of the building. He stopped and took his phone from his pocket, switching on its torch. It was pitch black and with the fog acting as a shield he thought it a risk worth taking. The clump of trees and bushes which marked the location of the grave made odd silhouettes and when a figure in a hat appeared to be watching him he stopped dead in his tracks until he realised it was the branch of a tree swaying in the breeze. He moved off the path and found Tommy's stone.

He knelt down and shook off his bergen. He took out a tarpaulin, collapsible shovel and a head lamp. From one of the side pockets he removed the knitting needles.

He knelt down and pushed a needle into the ground at each of the stone's four corners and then spread the tarpaulin out to one side. He picked up the shovel and prepared to use it to lever up the stone.

For a second doubt crept in. Had this really been placed there by Tommy? What if it was the grave of a person whose identity he had stolen? Hardly anyone he had been investing in the Kieran Wells murder had been operating under their real names. But the inscription gave dates that could be linked to McCole. Never accept coincidences. Always check them out. He made a decision and reached for the head light.

Then his brain registered a sound that shouldn't have been present. He stopped what he was doing and remained perfectly still. The fog seemed to distort and muffle noise but it sounded like a vehicle was coming slowly up the church driveway. He could definitely hear the crunch of gravel.

He crouched for a moment, looking for the probe of headlights piercing the fog. He could see nothing but whatever it was was getting closer.

Batt's instinct told him that in this situation the best form of defence was attack. He grabbed the shovel and one of the knitting needles and followed the path round to the other side of the church. Keeping close to the building he reached the front corner. About halfway down the drive he thought he could make out the shape of a van. His ears picked up the sound of the engine ticking as it cooled.

For a while nothing seemed to happen. Then the doors opened – driver's side first then the passenger's - and the interior light came on. Two shadowy figures dropped to the ground and the passenger moved round to the same side as the driver.

Batt steadied his breathing and stood watching in the shadows. Professional hit-men would not have allowed the interior light to come on. He began to relax a little.

Then there was the whisper from a male voice followed by a giggle from a female. He heard the rear side door open and then close behind them. He let the tension drain from his neck and shoulders. Clearly he wouldn't be troubled for a while.

Back at the grave he replaced the needle, wedged the spade under the stone and used a fallen branch to help lever it up. He wondered whether to risk using his head torch. It was important not to leave any loose soil lying around once he'd done what he had to do. He couldn't see the corner of the church let alone the van so put the strap around his head and switched on.

He moved the stone and placed it on the tarpaulin before returning to where it had lain and starting to dig. The ground was fairly moist under the bushes, despite the recent hot weather. Each spadeful of earth was placed carefully on the sheet. He wasn't sure how far down he needed to dig. He thought thirty centimetres was probably more than enough. He expected to hit something solid at that depth but there was nothing.

He went a little deeper. Still nothing. He felt in his bergen for another knitting needle and pushed it into the ground at the bottom of the hole. About half way down the needle stopped. He pulled it out and pushed it in again at another spot. Same result. The needle went in the same distance before making contact with something solid.

He resumed digging and was finally able to scrape away the earth from the top of what looked like a wooden box. Brushing the last of it away with his hand, his light reflected off a brass plaque. He quickly set to work loosening the casket from where it was buried and lifted it out. It felt heavy. He gave it a gentle shake and heard a sound like gravel.

He wasn't going to waste any time trying to undo the brass screws that secured the lid, even though he'd brought a screwdriver along. He picked up the shovel and scooped the earth back in before moving the stone in order to shake the last pieces off the tarpaulin. The soil didn't quite fill the hole but it didn't matter – the stone would cover it. Anyway he would be back in a few weeks with Tommy's ashes.

The stone once more back in position, he pulled up the needles and put them, the casket, tarpaulin and shovel back into his bergen. He used the head torch to check everything was as he had found it, and then switched off.

As far as he knew, the van hadn't moved. He had to pass it if he was going to head back to his car. Was it worth the risk? He'd give it five minutes. There wasn't any particular hurry but he had work in the morning.

He again edged around the back of the church and down the side until he could just make out the van's profile. He dropped to his haunches and waited. He wondered whose name was on the casket's lid. It surely had to be Tommy's. He was tempted to take it out of his bergen and have a look, but it was too risky. He wondered why Tommy had chosen a C. of E. churchyard rather than a Catholic one. He supposed it didn't matter – his mortal remains hadn't been buried, at least not yet. Would he be bothered when they were finally laid to rest? Thinking about it Batt realised that McCole wouldn't be the only Catholic buried in St. Leonard's. The oldest graves dated from the time when England had been a Catholic country. King Henry, he reckoned, had a lot to answer for. Well, he along with one of his successors, William of Orange.

His ears picked up the sound of the van's side door sliding open. The happy couple emerged perhaps with satisfied expressions on their faces but he was not able to confirm it because of the fog that was now cutting visibility down to twenty or so metres. He heard two muffled bangs as both front doors closed and then the engine started.

Batt ducked into the shadows as the headlights came on and the van moved forwards in his direction. The lights swept over and past him as the driver did a three point turn in front of the main doors and headed off down the drive and into the night. He tightened the bergen's straps around his waist and chest and moved off in the same direction, once again keeping to the grass verge.

He was soon back on the lane and heading towards where he had left his car. It was an old habit that made him stop a short distance from it and check that everything seemed normal.

No faint smell of a cigarette or deodorant. No twigs snapping underfoot.

He took a deep breath and carried on walking, pulling out his key fob from his pocket and pressing the unlock button as he went. He took one last look behind him and quickly pulled open the rear door. No-one was sitting there with a loaded pistol aimed at his head. He unclipped his bergen and slung it onto the seat before opening the driver's door and getting ready to set off back to Bishops Bromley.

It was slow going at first but, once he'd left the Peak District behind, the fog became less dense and he was able to pick up speed, arriving home in the early hours.

With the events of the last few days he felt he was suffering from sleep deprivation. His first shift back at work started at ten o'-clock but, much as he wanted to see what Tommy's casket contained, he put off opening it and went to bed.

Chapter 15

The drive to Burton the next morning was slow going. An accident in the fog at Newborough the previous evening meant traffic was still being diverted down the country lanes. A car had mounted the verge and brought a telegraph pole down. The vehicle was at the side of the road waiting to be towed away and Batt could see the amber flashing lights of a couple of Open Reach vans in the middle of the road as engineers set about erecting a new pole.

The town centre was in its usual gridlocked state and so by the time he had parked up in the police compound he only had minutes to spare before briefing. The casket was out of sight in the boot, and he had deliberately parked where he could see the car from the office window. Not that he expected any trouble. The IRA's interest appeared to have ended with the shooting of Quinn, and as far as he was aware O'Brien knew nothing about the casket.

Pete James was waiting for him at reception. He tapped his watch and grinned.

'Morning George. Good to have you back.'

He held out a plastic jiffy bag.

'Your warrant card.'

He signed in and together they climbed the stairs and walked down the corridor to Conference Room B. When they entered all eyes turned towards them. Batt felt uncomfortable with the attention. There was a moment's silence which had him wondering whether he was welcome any more, and then he was surrounded by smiling faces and made to listen to everyone's words of support. Even DI Mills seemed genuinely pleased to see him back.

Pete led the briefing, outlining any progress teams had made with ongoing investigations and bringing everyone up to speed with new cases.

Mills's Green team was to concentrate on following up leads on a series of thefts from town centre warehouses, with Mills himself being tasked with writing a final report on the murder of Kieran Wells before it was officially declared a cold case. Batt's Blue team was to continue to take statements from members of the public who were complaining about hate crimes but, except for cases judged to be potentially serious, they were to begin a fresh crackdown on the local drugs scene.

The meeting broke up after a few questions had been answered and Batt met up with his three colleagues back at their office.

They had coffee whilst Batt was brought up-to-date with things. Helen had finally managed to get Elsie Goodbody to Citizens Advice, and she and Baz had already been given a couple of useful tip-offs by Ben Rogers. On the strength of that he asked them to take the lead on tackling the local drugs scene, until he and Chris Talbot had worked their way through the remaining hate crimes accusations.

During the course of the day he was able to write several reports based on notes his team had made, ready for the CPS to study. Chris had been out and about interviewing several people accused of racial discrimination, and one employer who had been accused of sexual harassment. Before their shift had ended the two of them had reviewed these latest cases and prioritised them for further investigation.

Batt had stopped off on the way home to get some shopping and it had gone 7:00pm by the time he pulled up onto the parking space at the back of his house.

He had noticed the mobile fish and chip van outside one of the pubs as he had driven down the village's main street and decided it would be quicker to get his dinner from there rather than waste time cooking. He wanted to see what was in the casket.

With fish, chips and peas steaming on his plate he ran outside and took the box from the boot of his car. He returned to the house, locked the door and set about cleaning the brass plaque so he could read the inscription. It simply read *Tommy McCole b.4 June 1946 d.3 March 2024.*

With one hand loading his fork and the other holding a screwdriver he set to work.

The four screws came out without any trouble. He put down his fork, pulled off the lid and peered inside. The box had a lead lining and inside was a package wrapped in oilskin sitting on a bed of what looked like sharp-sand.

He took a few more mouthfuls of dinner, allowing himself time to let relief sink in. He'd made the correct call. What he had dug up was not someone's ashes but something Tommy had planted there. Had he originally intended that someone to be a member of the IRA and had had a last-minute change of mind? There was no way of telling, of course, but he'd entrusted the contents to Batt presumably in the hope he'd do the right thing with them.

He pushed his plate to one side and carefully lifted the package out, placing it gently on the table. The oilskin had been secured with tape and had to be cut with a pair of scissors. The incision opened up to reveal a couple of books, each in a plastic ziplok bag.

He carefully removed the first one and shook the sand from it. He took it out of the plastic bag and read the title: 'Green Book'. It was the IRA's bible that was issued to all recruits.

He flicked through the pages and saw sections dealing with their aims and training methods. Turning to the first page he noted the early text referred back to "The Democratic Programme of the First Dial" which, Batt learned, was drawn up shortly after the Sinn Fein victory in the 1918 elections and which supported a united Ireland. It was the bedrock of the IRA's justification for its campaign of violence.

He skipped a few pages and read,

"The Irish Republican Army, as the legal representatives of the Irish people, are morally justified in carrying out a campaign of resistance against foreign occupation forces and domestic collaborators. All volunteers are and must feel morally justified in carrying out the dictates of the legal government, they as the Army are the legal and lawful Army of the Irish Republic which has been forced underground by overwhelming forces".

The text that followed made the recruits aware that the British Army was an occupying force and that the RUC, Garda, UDR and Free State Army were illegal armies and illegal forces who were morally wrong and politically unacceptable.

He paused for a moment and wondered about the extent to which teaching in schools had helped condition young Catholics to accept this.

He turned to the next page and the first words were,

"The Army as an organisation claims and expects your total allegiance without reservation."

This was followed by a statement which made him shudder.

"When volunteers are trained in the use of arms they must fully understand that guns are dangerous, and their main purpose is to take human life, in other words to kill people, and volunteers are trained to kill people."

Thoroughly engrossed, he read on and learnt how the IRA's policy had taken a decisive turn in 1969.

"In 1969 the existing conditions dictated that Brits were not to be shot, but after the Falls curfew all Brits were to the people acceptable targets."

1969 would probably have been the time Tommy had joined up. Batt thought back to the conversation they had had whilst out fishing for the day on Blithfield Reservoir. McCole had spoken bitterly about the Falls Road curfew and the way the community had been treated by the British Army.

There then followed an explanation about a change in strategy to guerrilla warfare. The explanation was that a 'hit and run' policy was needed which caused as many casualties and deaths of enemy personnel as possible, whilst at the same time making the enemy's financial interest in the Provinces unprofitable. This must have been the time when Tommy had gained his bomb-making expertise.

After putting forward explanations and reasons for the killing of what it called "the enemy", the Green Book turned to giving advice centred around anti-interrogation techniques. Batt read with interest the IRA's descriptions of physical and psychological torture its members might expect if arrested, and of the Army's use of humiliation. It was not too dissimilar to what he had been taught before going out to Afghanistan with the Paras.

"Interrogation is only necessary when the interrogator is unaware of information. The best anti-interrogation is to SAY NOTHING."

The Green Book concluded with the instruction "*say nothing, sign nothing, see nothing, hear nothing.*" and the warning that if any member gave away information "*we execute informers*".

Batt realised this was what O'Brien and Tommy had been referring to when they had spoken about "the death sentence".

He closed the book. From what he had read it seemed remarkably professional. However, it had been written in the 1970s. Had the Green Book been updated when the IRA made the decision to take the campaign to the mainland, he wondered. Perhaps that was what was in the second ziplok bag.

He got up and washed his plate and made himself another coffee. Perhaps Tommy had had an input into a revised Green Book. After all, he had been the IRA's Quartermaster on the mainland. He took his drink back into the dining room and took the second book out of the oilskin wrapper.

It was not a book but as small ring binder. He opened it at the first sheet.

McCole had attached to it a letter addressed to him from the Executive Council. It outlined the reason for his posting to England. An IRA unit made up of Martin O'Connell, Eddie Butler, Harry Duggan and Brendan Dowd had been arrested following a long and successful series of operations and sentenced at the Old Bailey in 1977. There were fears that arrests of other operatives, including the Quartermaster, were imminent. New faces were necessary on the mainland. McCole had been selected to head up the new teams. His appointment would begin in May of 1977 and he would be based in Derbyshire. His cover was that he was the owner of a photographic studio in Bakewell.

What followed this letter was the first page of an A-Z of names together with faint annotations and some contact-sized photographs. In all there were seven pages. Batt wondered who these people were. They sounded Irish with names like Byrne, Donnelly, Geoghan, Kennedy, McGee, O'Sullivan and Ward.

He got up and returned with a magnifying glass and torch.

The annotations had been written in pencil and were beginning to fade. He looked through the sheets to find the best preserved and, with magnifier in one hand and torch in the other he managed to read *"Arr 7/89. Dev Team. Flashgun. Deale. Gow, Terry. Downing. Paddington. Victoria. Baltic. Warrington. Bishopsgate. Ret May 94."*

Batt fired up his laptop and searched for the name of the man Tommy had written notes about. Nothing came up. He tried each of the entries in turn. The last two, Warrington and Bishopsgate, both had one thing in common – IRA bombings. He entered all of the words he knew to be place names and got the same result – IRA bombings.

He was left with Gow and Terry. A further internet search informed him Ian Gow had been a Conservative MP who had been killed in 1990 by a bomb placed under his car. Sir Peter Terry had been a Governor of Gibraltar and he and his wife had been seriously wounded in what was thought to have been an IRA attack on them at their home in Milford Common on the edge of Cannock Chase. Tommy McCole had spoken about it, he remembered.

It seemed the A-Z list of names was possibly a directory of the IRA personnel who had been under McCole's direction in England.

Batt realised he was starting to sweat. If this was what he thought it was then, in the wrong hands, its value was off the scale. He wondered who the wrong hands might be. Perhaps not the obvious ones.

He read through the names again, looking for any he recognised and came across that of Patrick Sheehy. Tommy had told him how the IRA's Sheehy had taken his own life because of his feeling of guilt for killing a man in London.

He read what he could of the notes against the name.

'Arr 1987. Button man 3. Unit 2. 1 kill 1988 London. Ret 1987. d. 1991 Suicide.'

There were a few other words he couldn't decipher

He ran another internet check and what he read confirmed the entry in McCole's directory.

What, he wondered, was contained in the rest of the folder. He turned the pages until he came to the next section. It was another A-Z, but this time the names were of those belonging to the government, MI5, Special Branch and the RUC, Ian Gow, Sir Peter Terry, Maurice Oldfield, Christopher Tugendhat, Francis Pym, Humphrey Atkin and Margaret Thatcher amongst them. Batt counted over forty entries, the intelligence on each being comprehensive.

He didn't want to read any more. He didn't want to know what Tommy McCole had been involved in. He only wanted to know the man he had befriended in the care home, not a man with a violent past.

But he was like a child who covered his face with his hands so as not to see, but who couldn't stop himself peering through his fingers.

He turned more pages. The list of names stopped and he came to a sort of scrap book with photographs and sheets of paper written in various hands.

They were accounts of IRA activities: the attacks on Ian Gow and Sir Peter Terry, the Greenwich Gas Works, the Royal Overseas Club, Downing Street, the Carlton Club, the Stock Exchange, Paddington Station, Victoria Station, the Baltic Exchange,the Warrington shopping centre and The Grand Hotel in Brighton. Each began with a list of equipment that had been requested by the IRA unit or individual. Sometimes Tommy had noted the initials of those involved but more often than not it was clear he had no prior knowledge of either those involved or of their intended target. There were reports for each entry, written presumably by those involved, assessing the result each attack. Occasionally Tommy had scribbled a few comments about the suitability of the target or of the devices and weapons used. At the end of several of the reports he had underlined the words "warning given but not acted upon".

It was the last of these accounts that Batt read in its entirety. It was about the Brighton bombing that had so nearly killed the Prime Minister, Margaret Thatcher.

Early in 1984 McCole had been asked to supply a driving licence in the name of Roy Walsh (which McCole had noted, he had challenged as it was the name of an IRA bomber already serving a life sentence in prison), a car, £500 in cash, 100lbs of Semtex and a 30-day timing device. Tommy had also challenged the amount of Semtex on the grounds that supplies were running very low. He was to make the drop on 26th August to a safe house in Dagenham.

Batt turned to the bomber's report. It was dated 19th October 1984.

Materials received as requested. Recce comp on 12th Sept. No early security preps for conference evident. No obvious surveillance. Booked room at Grand for seven nights. Changed appearance – beard gone. Destroyed passport and cleaned up at Dagenham. Drove to Brighton and left car in The Dials area. Caught bus to hotel.

Checked in to Grand on 14th. Signed in using Roy's name. Tried to be careful not to leave prints on the card but had to hand back to reception – might be a problem if card is kept for a few weeks. Spoke with my Norwich accent. Was allocated

Room 629. Carried my own cases. Good position – rooms above, below and to the side. Found ideal place to leave package – managed to unscrew bath panel and hide under bath. Set timer for 24 days – 12th Oct. during Conference week. Did clean sweep of room and checked out on 19th. Kept Grand under surveillance. Security tightened from 7th Oct. No sign of dogs being used. Delegates arriving from 9th onwards. Left for home on 10th.

Successful detonation. Early reports of 5 dead, 30+ injured. Thatcher survived. Major damage to Grand.

Wish to return to England to continue to target coastal hotels.'

It had been signed 'PM' and dated 14th October 1984.

McCole had added an update about Magee's subsequent arrest.

"Bombing of government figures sent shockwaves and fear amongst public. Special Branch greatly increased protection of leading politicians and physical deterrents constructed around key buildings.

In 1985 Pat given approval by Security Council to return to mainland to conduct new bombing campaign. I received a copy of his letter of consent, which made it clear that another Warrington was to be avoided at all costs and that civilian targets were off limits. Warnings had to be given in time for areas to be cleared. Peter Sherry was sent to join him in England to lend his expertise.

Pat's campaign was set to begin in June using same timing device as the one at Brighton.

Detonations set for July and August. Target hotels = mainly in south.

Sources have since told me they now think Sherry had been under constant surveillance by Special Branch. Seems he was tailed from Carlisle to Glasgow railway station and from there to Queens Park where Cell 6 was gathered. Pat had already arrived from his base in London. It was he who opened the door when Special Branch knocked. All arrested. Pat's schedule of bombings plus his diagrams of detonating devices were seized.

Rubens Hotel in London was first on his hit list. Pat had already placed the device there and SB linked it to him through his fingerprints on a reception card. The bomb was diffused despite it having one of our latest mercury tilt switches and a micro switch. His stache of explosives was found in the cellar of a nearby hotel in James Grey Street.

Police later revealed through the media that they had already been on to Pat. They had eliminated all but one of the people who had completed registration cards for room 629 at The Grand in the 14 weeks before the attack. The remaining card, signed in the name of Roy Walsh, had a fingerprint on it. The print matched one already held on file from when Pat had been arrested as a teenager when he had been living in Norwich. Unfortunate and bad luck.

Pat is now in the Maize prison, spending his time working towards a Doctorate as well as passing on his knowledge to fellow members."

There was one last note, added at a later date, which read simply " *Pat Magee released from Maize in Aug 1999 following Good Friday Agreement.*"

Batt leaned back in his chair and let out the breath he found he had been holding. What he had in his hands was a detailed history of the IRA's bombing campaign in England, complete with names, dates and places – even the bombers' appraisals of how their missions had gone.

He was tempted to read through the other accounts but perhaps the less he knew the better. The Brighton bombing was now well documented, but the others weren't.

There were the last few pages in the folder to look at. Then he had to decide what to do with it. What would Tommy want? He thought he perhaps knew.

He got up and stretched. It was beginning to get dark. He made himself another coffee and returned to his seat.

The last sheets in the folder were plastic wallets containing photographs. He counted fourteen in total.

The first was of a group of five, seated around a table. Tommy had written their names under each of them: Desmond O'Malley, Gerry Adams, Charles Haughey and Albert Reynolds. It was dated 1992.

The next was of a group of men posing outside in what looked like a prison exercise yard. Brendan Hughes, Tom McFeeley, Sean McKenna, Leo Greene, Tommy McKearney and John Nixon. They were wearing ordinary clothes and had hands raised in V for Victory signs. It was dated 24th October 1980.

Photograph three was dated June 1972. Batt recognised three of the four men: Martin McGuiness, Sean MacStiofain and Seamus Twomey.

He never got further than the next picture. It was a group dressed in paramilitary uniforms, their faces covered by balaclavas or scarves. Tommy had named them, though. At the back were James Drumm, Martin McGuinness, Gerry Adams and Seamus Twomey. Kneeling in front of them holding carbines and rifles were Michael Flynn, a young Tommy McCole, Packie McWilliams and Andrew Kennedy.

Packie McWilliams was, according to Quinn, the man he had murdered at Fairview Mansions, the man who was an undercover agent working for British Intelligence – Kieran Wells. He picked up his magnifying glass and studied the image. The height might have matched but it was difficult to judge from the man's kneeling position. Without being able to see the face it was difficult to tell whether Wells could once have been McWilliams.

He looked at their weapons. Between them they carried quite a formidable arsenal of Armalites. Flynn held an AR-18 rifle, the 'Widowmaker' as it was known. Tommy and McWilliams had AR-180 semi automatic rifles cradled in their arms. He looked at Kennedy's which was held vertically. It looked to Batt as though it was an AR-50 long range sniper rifle. Which version was it? Batt felt he ought to know. He had gained something of a reputation in Afghanistan for supplying accurate intelligence on weaponry. He looked again through the magnifying glass.

It wasn't the gun he recognised, though. It was the man holding it. The man with his little finger missing.

And suddenly he knew. Knew who had betrayed Kieran Wells and Tommy McCole. And why.

Two people. One to flush out his would-be assassin and the other to keep his political ambitions on track. O'Brien and Batt's IRA interrogator working as a team.

He picked up the folder and went outside. He lit the gas on the barbeque and burnt everything until only grey ash was left. The casket he would keep for when he buried

Tommy's remains and the photograph he had taken from his room on the night of his death.

Post Script

It was an autumn morning that Keats would have loved and Batt was in his workshop hunched over the disassembled movement of a longcase clock. Siobhan appeared at the door with a piece of toast and cup of coffee on a tray for him.

'Here,' she said. 'Breakfast. The most important meal of the day.'

He looked up and put the wheel he was cleaning down on the bench.

'Sleep well?'

'Like a corpse. That bed is really comfortable.'

'I know. I've used it myself on occasion.'

He looked at a card that still lay on the tray.

'If that's from Nick at G-Tec tell him I don't want a cordless mower, vacuum cleaner, hedgecutter…'

'No it's not from Nick. Here.'

She put down the tray and put the postcard face down on the bench.. Batt glanced over at it.

'It's a picture of a cow,' he said impatiently.

'It's not a cow, it's a bull. A Hereford bull according to the card.'

She turned it over.

'No message. Just two kisses on the bottom.'

Author's Note

Many of the IRA attacks mentioned in this book did take place, and many of the names I have used of those associated with the IRA are well documented.

Maurice Oldfield, the Head of MI5, did spend much of his time at the family farm in Derbyshire and by all accounts was fairly relaxed about his personal security, despite attempts by the IRA to frighten or kill him. He was included in "Who's Who", his occupation given as Head of MI5, and his mother's phone number was actually listed in the local directory.

Names that will not appear in public records of events associated with The Troubles include Tommy McCole, Brendan Quinn, Packie McWilliams and Andrew Kennedy.

The extracts from the IRA's Green Book are genuine. A version of the book is available online for a touch over £20.

www.ingramcontent.com/pod-product-compliance
Ingram Content Group UK Ltd.
Pitfield, Milton Keynes, MK11 3LW, UK
UKHW020005160325
456262UK00006B/419

9 781917 601849